In CROSSING LINES, the world's best-stocked toy drawer can only take a gal so far. Bored with her current assortment of vibrating, plastic pieces, building inspector Sam Wallace decides to add a new sex toy to her collection: Kevin Mazze. The irresistible Italian is happy to help her live out her long-held sexual fantasies, while also insinuating himself into her life and winning the affection of her five-year old daughter. But just as Sam starts to trust Kevin with her heart, as well as her body, she learns he's committed an unforgivable sin.

Myrtle Beach developer Kevin Mazze is one of the good guys. He's spent his life always doing the right things and making those around him happy, even if it means maintaining a relationship long after it's reached its expiration date. When he meets the woman of his dreams, he finds himself making bad choices in the name of good and crossing lines he never thought he would… while praying she never learns of the secret he's been hiding.

Crossing Lines

Book #3 in the Heat Wave Series

Alannah Lynne

Dedication

To Dusty and Grey

You guys are my sun and moon.

There are no words to tell you how much I love you both!

Acknowledgements

There are so many people who help me get a book ready to go. I usually forget someone (even though I keep a running list of everyone I want to thank), and I'm so sorry for that!

Thank you to Jeff Mosley for helping me make Kevin's life hell. Jeff was so full of great ideas, I had a hard time keeping up with him as he rattled off possible scenarios. The biggest problem I had was getting him to help me figure out a way to get Kevin out of hot water!

Also, thanks to Cheri Biddix for helping me brainstorm Lizbeth's career choice. I still have the massive string of texts on my phone! We really should've gone to lunch. LOL

Not too far into this writing process, I realized Kevin spoke Italian when he was "thinking out loud" and didn't want anyone to know what he said. The problem is I'm not Italian and I know nothing about the language. As is the case anytime I need help, the universe sent me an angel. Thank you, Marianne Strnad, for all of your help and for always responding to my questions so quickly. I can't wait to finally meet you.

Prior to "meeting" Cassie McCown, I considered editing a grueling process and dreaded it more than just about anything (except writing the synopsis or the back cover copy). No more! I thoroughly enjoy working with Cassie and am always a little sad when the book is finished. Thank you for helping me bring the books to life and for making the editing process so enjoyable!

As always, a massive thank you to Violet Duke for an amazing cover and brand!

When I started the self-publishing journey, I felt like I needed a board of directors. A group of ladies who believed in me and enjoyed my books, but who wouldn't blow smoke up my ass and tell me what I wanted to hear. I needed honest direction. I am so blessed to have picked four ladies I love dearly, who do an amazing job of helping me with any and every little thing I need. Cheri Biddix, Liz Henderson, Michelle Unger, and Amanda McFarland. THANK YOU!

Last but certainly not least, a huge, MASSIVE thank you to my street team!! Alannah's Beach Angels are the coolest, sweetest, kindest and most giving group of ladies I've ever been blessed to know. You bring so much joy to my life. You make me laugh, and sometimes tear up, with your personal stories. You are so welcoming to new members, and I can't tell you how much I appreciate all of your pimping efforts. You guys are the best!

Chapter One

Can this day get any worse?

Flipping fate the bird with a taunting question was foolish, but Kevin Mazze couldn't help himself as he glared down at the pixie standing between him and the grand opening of his exclusive subdivision.

Dieci, nove, otto, sette…

Why bother counting backward from ten to try and diffuse his anger? Rather than calming him, he always felt he counted down to an explosion.

Take now, for example. The pulse pounding in his temples suggested if he kept going, his head would explode, splattering fragments all over the pavement.

The up side was it would also make a mess of the petite, blond building inspector threatening to not only ruin his day, but his whole fucking year.

Stopping the countdown before he reached detonation, he scrubbed a hand across his forehead, then slowly and plainly said, "I need the Certificate of Occupancy. Without it, I'm dead in the water." Okay, talking to her as if she were deaf and dumb probably wouldn't gain him any favors—

Annnddd, there it went. The squashing of hope, along with a quick tightening in his stomach as he prepared for another swift kick in the nuts. She slammed her hands to her hips and squared her shoulders, pulling herself up to a truly impressive height of five foot one. If the situation weren't so dire, and she didn't hold his entire career in the palm of her hand, he would laugh. He might even get a little turned on, because her feisty back-at-ya attitude was sexy as hell.

"Is your hearing defective, Mr. Mazze? Or are you just a little slow on the uptake? I know you need a CO. But you don't have enough water pressure to operate the sprinklers." Mirroring his speech pattern, she slowed her cadence so even a first grader would understand. "You're not occupying the building until the problem is solved."

Several things kept his hands fisted at his sides rather than wrapped around her pretty little neck. One, she was a woman. Two, she was right.

She wasn't responsible for the county's negligence in following through with the promised water tower that would provide the pressure necessary for powering the sprinklers. Ultimately, the responsibility for this massive failure lay squarely on his shoulders.

His father insisted on taking the gamble and jumping the gun with this project. Kevin recognized the risk from the beginning, but he'd acquiesced to his father's wishes. Now, while Papà visited family in Italy, reliving his childhood, Kevin was left with a mop and dry bucket, figuring out how to clean up the mess.

"I've been on the phone with Public Works every day for ten days," he said, hoping to appeal to her sense of reasoning since his attempts at charming aggression had gotten him nowhere. "They said the tower would be up and running in another few weeks."

Of course, the bastards promised that six months ago, too, and he still hadn't seen any evidence of progress. But Samantha Wallace was new in town, so maybe she didn't know how badly the county dragged their feet. Relaxing his posture, he gave her a stretched, confident smile and prayed she bought the massive pile of bullshit.

She cocked her head to the side and smiled, indicating a shortage of spending cash. Despite the ominous black clouds rolling in, she still wore her sunglasses, which prevented him from seeing her eyes. Pity, because based on her smile's amperage, he'd bet her eyelashes were fluttering like crazy behind those mirrored lenses. "I may be blond, Mr. Mazze, but I'm not an idiot."

After snapping the words like a whip, emphasizing her unwillingness to back down, she crossed her arms over her chest and glanced away. Her sharp exhale and creased forehead projected her sympathy, the show of regret doing more to diffuse his anger than counting backward from a thousand.

Despite her reputation for being a hardnosed bitch, she wasn't busting his balls to be difficult. Code dictated what she could and couldn't do, and in this case, her hands were tied.

An image of her naked, hands bound, kneeling on his bed, flashed through his mind. He had no explanation for the inappropriate thought, but this obviously wasn't the time or place for his junkyard dog to wake up and fight against his chain.

He shook his head to clear the thought and leaned against the landscaper's bumper. He worked his neck in a circle, finally looking to the heavens for guidance. An answering flash of lightning wasn't reassuring.

"You have any suggestions?" he asked Wade Neumann, the job foreman, who'd been standing off to the side, silently watching the drama unfold.

"No, sir. I've never dealt with anything like this." Wade sighed and his shoulders drooped. "I'm sorry."

"Not your fault, bro. Papà and I took the gamble." A huge, *pricey* gamble that might set Kevin back years.

In a perfectly coordinated display of I'll-show-you, lightning flashed and thunder shook the ground at the exact moment his cell phone erupted with the theme from *Psycho*.

"*Yes,*" Fate cackled. "*I can fuck your day up a little more.*"

Wade's mouth twitched, but as a smart young man concerned with job security, he bit down on his lip and squelched his grin.

Far superior and unconcerned with job security, Samantha Wallace flashed a grin brighter than the lightning. "Nice," she said with a husky little laugh. "I should use that for my ex."

Kevin didn't correct her assumption Lizbeth was an ex. He also didn't answer the call.

"Unless you wait for the water tower,"—she cast him a pointed look—"which won't be up in the next two weeks, the only thing you can do is put in a booster pump." At his muttered curse, she lifted a shoulder and gave a regretful shake of her head. "I know you don't want to take the additional cost on the chin, but I don't see any other option." She threw her hands up animatedly. "Hell, even if I gave you the CO, the fire marshal would swoop in here and shut your ass down before you cut on the first light."

Frustration chomped at the back of his throat, begging to break free with a growl and a massive curse. What the hell was he supposed to do at—he glanced at his watch—four o'clock on a Friday?

"*Shit!* It's four o'clock."

Wade and the building inspector exchanged glances at his outburst. One of her blond eyebrows lifted, and Wade answered with a shrug.

To Wade, he said, "I'm supposed to be in Riverside in two hours." To Samantha, who didn't appear to understand his predicament, he said, "I have a three-and-a-half-hour drive, besides a stop in Anticue to check on the progress of a restaurant. Needless to say, I'm real fucking late." He winced. "Sorry, excuse the coarse language."

He hadn't intended to be funny, but she found something about his apology hilarious. Her braid swung side to side when she tossed her head back and laughed from deep in her chest, making him wonder if her hair was as soft as it looked.

He also found himself oddly curious about the color of her eyes and wanted to demand she take those damned shades off so he could see. Based on her fair skin and nearly white hair, he figured blue.

A sweet baby-blue.

While he stared like a dumbstruck moron, she said, "I'm the last person you need to apologize to for cursing. You know how when someone quits smoking, they'll gravitate to other smokers so they can inhale the secondhand toxic waste? Well, that's me with cussing." She waved off her copious explanation. "Never mind. Have a safe trip."

Caught in the moment of seeing her as a beautiful woman, not the building inspector shitting on his parade, it took a while for him to realize his phone was ringing. Again.

He unclipped it from his belt and wrestled with the urge to toss the thing in the retention pond. Instead, he hit the silence button, then stuck his hand out as a peace offering. "I'm sorry for being an ass. Can we...?" When she placed her palm in his, heat from the contact washed over him, causing him to slip and nearly ask her to dinner. Fortunately, his brain reengaged and overrode the impulse. "Can we meet first thing Monday morning? I have to work this out."

Her soft, sympathetic smile conveyed her thoughts. *You poor, dumb son of a bitch. You just don't get it, do you?* But her mouth said, "Sure. Here or my office?"

"Here. I'll bring breakfast."

As he turned to leave, Wade asked, "Will you be back tomorrow?"

"Yep," he yelled over his shoulder. "I told Marianne I'd keep Spencer so she can have the day to herself."

"Enjoy your night, boss."

Yeah, right. Kevin waved to acknowledge Wade's comment, but didn't turn around. Instead, he pounded the pavement to his truck and recited his new mantra.

Two more weeks. Just two more weeks…

Chapter Two

*M*irrored shades served several functions. They looked cool. They protected the eyes. And they provided the perfect cover for sizing up a man's ass.

Sam Wallace always found work boots sexy, and as Kevin Mazze stormed across the parking lot, he screamed sex with a capital *S*. His powerful strides were like those of a lion as he moved with authorial grace through the concrete jungle he ruled, commanding attention and respect.

A sigh slipped from her lips as she followed the roll of his shoulders under his light-blue button-down shirt and the sway of the soft, well-worn denim.

He was the man her mama warned her about.

The one her friend, Cheri, begged her to find.

When angry, his eyes were cold and hard and his lips compressed into a sharp, thin line. But when he smiled, those steely eyes turned soft and gooey, like rich, dark chocolate, and his bottom lip grew thick and plump, perfect for nibbling.

The whole package reminded her of fresh-baked chocolate chip cookies, and her mouth watered for a bite.

She hadn't been with a man since her piece-of-shit ex walked out. And even though Cheri encouraged her to find one, Sam steadfastly refused. She didn't need a man… At least, that's what she claimed.

Kevin Mazze, however, put a little purr in her motor and made her want to take a test drive.

He wasn't wearing a ring—not that she'd been looking. She just happened to notice his finger was bare as he silenced his phone... Right before she saw the dark, curling chest hair peeking over the open top button of his shirt... Which she noticed when she snapped her gaze upward in an attempt to not get caught staring at his crotch... Which definitely snagged her attention.

Oh hell, who was she kidding? Everything about Mazze called to her on a deeply feminine level, guaranteeing him a starring role in all future fantasies.

"You'll have to overlook his irritability," Wade said, interrupting her thoughts. "He's on edge because of the wedding."

Her heart sank with the sound of screeching tires, signaling an end to her dreams before they even got started. "Oh, yeah? Who's the lucky girl?" Realizing that might come across more forward than she intended, she turned to Wade to clarify.

Before she could formulate her defense as nothing more than a figure of speech, Wade said, "Oh, no. I doubt Wildman will ever marry." He laughed nervously. "He's planning *my* wedding."

A ridiculous image of Mazze in a yellow sundress, wearing a matching hat and white gloves, directing the flower girl and bridesmaid from the back of a church, flashed through her mind. The scene was straight out of a bad horror movie and completely incongruous with the real-life, testosterone-driven flesh and blood.

The closest Mazze probably ever came to a dress was while removing one. Patience didn't seem his strong suit, so rather than dealing with delicate buttons or sticky zippers, she imagined he would just rip and strip.

Kinda makes a girl want to go out and buy a dress.

She removed her sunglasses and used her shirtsleeve to wipe the sweat from her eyes. "The heat must be getting to me. Did you say he was a wedding planner?"

Wade laughed and took off his ball cap. "Unfortunately, that's what's happened." He scratched the back of his head, then repositioned the cap a half dozen times before settling on a spot.

Looking at his boss with a combination of brotherly affection and hero worship, he said, "My fiancée wanted an outdoor wedding. Kevin's house in Riverside overlooks the Pamlico River… the perfect setting." He said the last in a singsongy voice as he made quotation marks with his fingers. "Kevin offered his house and now he's dealing with Lizilla—my fiancée's sister. She's an event planner and this is a great opportunity for her to do her thing. But she's driving everyone crazy. We'll be lucky if he and Lizbeth are still speaking when this is over." He kicked the curb. "We should've made life easy on everyone and eloped."

"I'd advise skipping the wedding altogether."

Wade grinned. "Bad first marriage?"

"Yeah, apparently."

Switching her attention to more important matters, she chewed the inside of her cheek and inspected the area surrounding the clubhouse, restaurant, and office. She pointed to a fresh-poured concrete slab in the back corner of the grouping. "Is that the dumpster pad?"

Wade nodded. "Yes, ma'am."

She pivoted on the heel of her boot and studied the parking lot and long, winding driveway. Working from memory of the site plan, she tried to envision where the waterline fed into the property.

Dread and regret for Mazze constricted her chest. Once open, this fly-in golf community along the Intracoastal Waterway would be spectacular. Until then, it was an expensive piece of property, racking up massive construction loan interest. Mazze needed, at bare minimum, to get the office operational so he could start selling lots and member-ships.

This hiccup would set him back weeks, if not months, and cost a fortune. Not only in the additional fees required to solve the problem, but also in lost income.

She'd been in Mazze's shoes, taking chances that landed her in this exact square on the builder's chessboard. He wasn't facing checkmate, but certainly a significant setback.

Only in Myrtle Beach a few months, she'd gained a reputation for being a bitch. She didn't like the moniker, but if her refusal to play by the good-ol'-boys' rules of overlooking code violations earned her the nasty name, she'd learn to live with it.

However, while she may be a bitch, she wasn't heartless.

She couldn't get him the Certificate of Occupancy if he didn't have operational sprinklers, but she might be able to help speed up the process. Not by a lot, but opening in two weeks rather than four could mean the difference in an annual profit or sinking into the red.

"I can't make any promises," she said, turning to Wade. "But I'll go back to the office, make some calls, and see what I can do."

His breath left in a whoosh as he extended his hand for a shake. "Thank you." He released his grip and reached into his back pocket for a cream-colored business card with black-and-gold lettering. "This has mine and Kevin's cell numbers. Call if you have any questions or need anything. Day or night, doesn't matter."

Well now, that certainly left a wide-open door to a room full of endless possibilities. No telling what she might need from Mazze in the deep of night.

She ran her thumb over his number and smiled. "I'll be in touch."

Kevin climbed into his truck, cranked the motor, and turned the A/C on full tilt. Myrtle Beach in September should be mid-eighties with reasonable humidity. Not hinges-of-hell hot with a humidity level so high it felt like the ocean packed up and moved inland.

He stared out the windshield as Samantha Wallace took off her sunglasses and wiped the sweat from her eyes. Dammit, why hadn't she done that earlier when he could steal a glimpse?

He leaned to the side so cold air from the vent blasted him in the face and gnawed on his lip while chewing his thoughts. Maybe the building inspector, not the weather, was the reason for his temperature spike.

Numerous rumors about her abounded, but she wasn't the ball-busting giant he expected. Hell, she wasn't any bigger than a minute.

He laughed and shook his head. His ass had been shut down by a *folletta.*

A feisty pixie wearing relaxed-fit jeans and a Horry County shirt that showed a lot of creamy cleavage when she threw her shoulders back and the buttons pulled tight.

She pivoted on her heel, which pulled his gaze to her beat-to-shit work boots. His boots were five years old and in rough shape. Hers were older and worse. She hadn't bought them specifically for this job, and he was intrigued by her work history.

Comfortable tromping through the mud without high stepping like most women, she'd obviously spent a lot of time on construction sites. And while standing her ground against him, she hadn't flinched.

The way she came at him with equal attitude was more of a turn-on than a high-dollar strip show. And when she bowed up and questioned his hearing, it took every ounce of self-restraint not to laugh.

Or kiss the shit out of her.

Make-up sex with her could become his favorite pastime.

As the daydream spiraled out of control, his overheated body drew taut and hardened, preparing for action, but his ringing phone broke the spell like an ice-cold bath would a fever. Without masking his anger or frustration, he answered. "What?"

"Bad day, darling?"

Lizbeth's sultry voice used to soothe him, but lately, especially on days like this, her slow drawl rankled his nerves and tightened the muscles in his neck and shoulders like a wrench. "Yeah, Lizbeth, not the best. You've called me fifteen times in the past hour. Someone better be on life support."

The sniff coming through the line painted a picture of her crimson lips pooched into a pout. He supposed he should feel bad and apologize for snapping, but his give-a-damn was busted, and he couldn't dredge up the energy to care.

"I haven't talked to you at all today and hardly any yesterday. I wanted to make sure you remembered tonight's party."

He exhaled in a slow, steady stream while willing his blood pressure to drop back into the safety zone. Fifteen calls to ask about a party? Good thing he hadn't interrupted his meeting to answer or he'd really need to apologize for a few foul, anger-laden words. Even in Italian, his intent would've broadcasted loud and clear.

He knew this would be the case, though, which was why he didn't even consider taking her earlier calls. Lizbeth was the girl who cried wolf. Everything was an emergency, assuring dire consequences if he didn't come to the rescue. Immediately.

In the beginning, the Mr. Fix-it in him liked being needed and enjoyed helping. After nearly two years of being on the job twenty-four-seven, Mr. Fix-it was tired and needed a break. He'd come to the conclusion it was time for a permanent leave of absence.

He just needed to figure out the right time to talk to Lizbeth… which wasn't two weeks before her sister's wedding.

"First off," he said, locking his jaw to temper his response, "the fundraiser is at my house. It'd be a little odd if I didn't show, don't ya think? Secondly, you and Kat have put a lot of effort into this fundraiser; it means a lot to you. Of course I'll be there."

His dedication to making an appearance had more to do with his loyalty to Kat than Lizbeth, but for once in his life, the filter responsible for keeping those kinds of comments unsaid actually worked.

"Thank you. I knew you wouldn't let me down. I… well, I wanted to hear your voice. Is that so bad?"

The weight of fatigue carried his head back until it landed with a thud against the headrest. He stared at the sun visor, then squinted, trying to read the scribbled, barely legible notes jammed everywhere. *Jesus, what a mess.* He really needed to clean his truck.

"No," he said, getting back online with the conversation. "Just bad timing. I have a serious problem with the new Vanguard development—"

"What time can I expect you?"

His temple gave a thump, warning him to lighten up on the teeth gnashing. He didn't know why he got angry since this was the way conversations normally went with her. No matter what he had going on, her issues always took precedence.

The stress of planning her sister's wedding and obsessing over every detail made her psychotic. At least, he hoped the wedding was to blame.

He'd hate to wake up and realize she'd been this way all along, and he'd been a blind, oblivious dumbass.

Rather than continuing the dead-end conversation, which would only keep him frustrated and make her whinier, he said, "I'll get there soon as I can," then disconnected the call without waiting for a response.

Man, he didn't want to do this. In a perfect world, he'd go home, grab a beer, hit the couch, and sleep thirty-six hours. But his world was light-years away from perfect, and what he wanted, at least right now, didn't matter. He needed to follow through on his commitments and get back to Riverside to a house full of people he didn't know. He sighed and his shoulders slumped so far forward he thought he might cave in on himself. He *needed* to get back to Lizbeth.

With one last glance to the little *folletta* who stormed onto the scene, disrupting his life in the most aggravating yet interesting way, he shoved the shifter into drive and pulled out of the lot.

Sam slid the piping-hot pizza box onto the kitchen counter, dropped her bag on the end table in the living room, then headed down the hall to her bedroom. Yelling over her shoulder to her five-year-old daughter, Michaela, she said, "Let me change and I'll be right there to get your pizza."

Five minutes later, she came back to a kitchen that smelled like the world's finest pizzeria and found Michy staring at the box like she could eat the pizza through osmosis.

"I'm starving, Mommy."

Sam slipped a slice of cheese pizza onto Michaela's plate before grabbing a slice of mighty meaty for herself. "I know, and I'm sorry I was late picking you up. I promise, next time I'll call and tell Ms. Kay so you won't be worried."

Running ten minutes behind was a serious and costly offense in the world of afterschool programs. However, neither the enormous late fee nor the lecture from the grumpy-faced director were the punch in the gut that left Sam aching for the past half hour.

That was compliments of her daughter.

Michy's eyes were still red-rimmed—not from crying, but from the extreme effort she'd exerted *not* crying. The poor thing even had teeth marks in her bottom lip from biting down to stop the quivering.

And that's why Sam nominated herself for the Mommy Fail of the Year Award.

Sam's little apple didn't fall far from the tree, and, like her mom, Michy would explode with pain or fear before she let her emotions escape in the form of tears.

"It's okay," Michy said through slurps of her soda. "I was just scared something bad happened."

Michaela started showing signs of insecurity after Sam's dad died. A year later, when Sam's piece-of-shit ex disappeared without a backward glance, Michaela turned into a leech. Her anxiety worsened with the move to Myrtle Beach, and Sam should've realized how severely her tardiness would affect Michy.

"Sweetie, you're the most important thing in the world to me. I would never just not show up."

The internal voice of black butterflies and stormy skies said, *You can't make those kind of promises. Your dad didn't* plan *on not showing up for work that morning.*

She growled, dismissing the doom-and-gloom thoughts once and for all, but Michy's reply only intensified the suffocating squeeze in her chest.

"I know. That's why I thought something bad happened."

"Yeah." Sam sighed. "I understand." She was glad Michy knew

she'd never voluntarily abandon her like the son of a bitch Michy called daddy. But she hated the lingering trauma her little girl suffered as a result of Papa's fatal heart attack and Michael's abandonment.

There was no way to reassure her daughter something like that wouldn't happen again. Heart attacks, car crashes, or the millions of other freak accidents that occurred on a daily basis didn't guarantee a girl wouldn't suddenly lose a parent. Or any loved one, for that matter.

As Michy grew up and started dating, Sam wouldn't be able to protect her and make sure she never had her heart broken. But she would do everything in her power to shelter and protect Michy as much as possible while she could, and hope, as a child, she never had to suffer another loss.

The late afternoon thunderstorms dropped the temperature, so Sam had traded her work clothes for sweat pants and a T-shirt. She glanced down at her fuzzy socks as she carried their plates to the living room.

Look at you. All dressed up and nowhere to go.

For the millionth time since leaving the Vanguard site, she thought of Kevin Mazze. An attractive, intelligent man like him probably spent his weekends attending extravagant parties or dining in upscale restaurants, surrounded by tall, thin supermodel types.

What would it take to get him interested in a short, curvy, less-than-glamorous mom, who spent her evenings at home, watching Disney movies, eating pizza, and drinking beer?

She was a lousy cook, so going by way of his stomach wasn't an option. Besides, she didn't want him on a permanent basis. She only wanted him for late-night extracurricular fun.

She glanced to the Vanguard Subdivision folder and site plan sitting with her bag. Maybe they could work something out in trade. She would help him figure out a solution to his problem, and he could show his gratitude by granting her a few dozen orgasms. How was that for sexy romance, guaranteed to drive a man wild?

"Of course I found someone else. Why wouldn't I find a real *woman?"*

Sam sucked in a breath and dropped to the sofa as Michael's words rushed at her, knocking her off her feet. She closed her eyes and gritted her teeth, determined to beat back the autopilot response that always insisted on replaying the entire tape.

Michaela, who had gone to her bedroom to get her pillow and blanket, ran to the sofa and crouched at Sam's feet. Peeking up from the floor, she asked, "Mommy? Are you okay?"

"I'm fine, sweetie. I just lost my balance and tripped." Sam drew in a ragged breath and set the paper plates on the old, worn-out coffee table that had fallen an inch short of the junkyard finish line. "Eat your pizza, and I'll get the movie ready."

Michy sat cross-legged in front of the coffee table and dove into her dinner while Sam carried tonight's Disney classic, *Beauty and the Beast,* to the DVD player.

"Can we go to the beach tomorrow?"

Bent over at the waist, disc in hand, Sam glanced over her shoulder. "Wow, what a shock. You want to go to the beach?"

Michy giggled and took a bite of her pizza. After sucking in a few quick breaths to cool her burning mouth, she said, "Yeah, but not to the part where we normally go. I want to go to the part that has the fierce wheel."

Sam grinned and finished loading the disc into the player. "A fierce wheel, huh? Since you don't even know what that is, why do you want to go there?"

Michy slurped her soda and wiped her mouth on her sleeve. "Because my friend Spencer's gonna be there."

Michaela met Spencer her first day at daycare, and the two became instant friends. For weeks, she asked if he could come over to play, but

Sam's path hadn't crossed with Spencer's mom's to make arrangements. With both of them being single moms, Sam even wondered if Spencer's mom might be interested in trading weekend babysitting so they each had some free time.

"Is it the fierce wheel at the boardwalk or the other one?" She grinned and winked. "It's a *Ferris* wheel,"—she narrowed her eyes and growled playfully—"not fierce like I'm going to get if you don't start using your napkin and stop ruining your shirts!"

"Yes, ma'am." Michy swiped at her face with the paper and thought for a minute. "He said something about walking."

Gee, that narrowed it down. She didn't want to burst her daughter's bubble, but finding Spencer at the Boardwalk on a Saturday wouldn't be easy. Granted, the middle of September wouldn't be nearly as crowded as a few weeks ago, but still…

Oh, what the hell. She didn't have anything pressing to do, and she wanted to talk to Spencer's mom anyway. If by some miracle they found them, it would give the two women a chance to talk. The thought of making new friends was damned appealing, and it wouldn't be a hardship to spend the day at the beach.

"Do you have any idea what time he's going?"

Michaela's face dropped and she shook her head.

"It's okay. We don't have anything else to do tomorrow. So if you'll let me sleep in for a while, then we'll head over there and see if we can find them. Okay?"

"Yay!" Michy grabbed Sam's leg and squeezed. "You're the best mommy, ever."

Sam grabbed the remote from the coffee table and flopped down on the sofa. "Even though I worried you?"

Finished with her pizza, Michy climbed onto the couch, snuggled against Sam's side, and pulled the blanket over her. "Yep. Still the best."

Sam smoothed back a rogue curl and rested her cheek on top of Michy's head. Wouldn't it be awesome to be five again, with the amazing power to forgive and especially forget so easily? She cut off the lamp beside the sofa and hit PLAY on the remote.

Since she wasn't five and she didn't seem able to ever let anything go, she was grateful for the opportunity to fly away to magical kingdoms, where even a beast had hope of finding happily ever after.

Chapter Three

*K*evin tugged at the tie cinched around his neck like a too-tight leash, desperate for relief from the suffocation that probably had more to do with his life, in general, than the piece of silk in his hand.

The coat and tie were bad, but he took a small measure of comfort in having been spared the cummerbund and bow tie. Point to Lizbeth for dialing back the *required* formality of tonight's affair. Most of the women, looking for a chance to relive their high school prom, chose to wear long cocktail gowns. Most of the men, probably also hoping to relive their proms by getting laid, went with less formal suits.

Erik Monteague, Kevin's closest friend and next-door neighbor, ambled over and stopped front and center. He wore his typical smartass smirk and his tone was like dry ice when he said, "Nice party."

"Only the best for my nearest and dearest," Kevin said, lifting his glass of shitty wine in salute to the room full of strangers before glancing at his watch. He'd gotten to Riverside as soon as possible, but with the stop in Anticue to check the progress of Gavin's restaurant, he was two hours late. Even though he had to listen to Lizbeth whine several more times on the phone, God willing, he'd only have two more hours of feeling like an outcast in his own home before he got out of the straight jacket and into a case of beer.

He studied Erik, just as out of place as Kevin, who somehow managed to appear suave and debonair... not like a sausage packed into a too-tight skin. Or a mob hit man.

At least half a dozen men had thrown their hands up in mock surrender and an equal number of women whispered inappropriate comments in his ear about his hidden gun.

Gotta love a party with free booze.

"Why aren't you turning blue and choking?"

Erik grinned and notched up his chin, showing off the top of his shirt. "Kat lets me leave the top button undone, then fixes the tie so you can't tell." He wagged his eyebrows as if to say, *Pretty smart, huh?*

His gaze wandered off in search of his pregnant wife. The moment he found her was obvious by the way his eyes softened and the corner of his mouth tweaked. She either met his stare or an eyelash slipped into his eye because he winked, then returned his attention to Kevin. "I know this isn't your kind of party, but thanks for helping raise funds for Saving Grace. The women's shelter means a lot to Kat."

Which was why Kevin had been more than happy to man up and play host, regardless of the dress code. Kat was the best thing that ever happened to Erik, and it wasn't much of a stretch to say she saved his life. For that reason, Kevin would be forever indebted and would go out of his way to make anything she wanted happen.

"No need to thank me. I just showed up. Lizbeth and Kat did all the work."

Giant topiaries embellished with large masks sat on either side of a fountain, which had, at some point during the week, been added to his foyer. Not for the first time, he wondered how they got the monstrous thing inside and made a mental note to check for a new entry door. Columns framed the wide front entry and he squinted in the dim light, trying to figure out… "Are those columns attached to the wall?"

Exasperated, he blew out a breath and took a quick gulp of wine, swallowing before the horrendous flavor had time to stick to the inside of his mouth and tarnish his taste buds. "How much is this get-together setting us back?"

Erik shrugged. "I have no idea." His head bounced side to side and his lips moved, like he was doing the math as he took in the details of the room. "I'd say close to a shitload."

When Lizbeth approached him about Mazze Builders underwriting the event, along with Monteague Boats, Kevin told her he'd be happy to. Now, he wondered if he should've asked a few more questions... and set a budget.

"This is all your fault," Erik said, nodding to the Venetian tapestry hanging on the wall and the upstairs balcony, which had been transformed into the Bridge of Sighs.

"Is that right?" Erik didn't elaborate, so Kevin did a quick run-through of possible offenses and decided the list was way too long to narrow down in one night, let alone a single conversation. "You're gonna have to be more specific."

Erik broke into a full-fledged grin that usually meant trouble—at least in the past, before he settled down and got in the family way—and took a sip of wine. Following a shudder, he said, "While kicking around possible themes, Lizbeth said they positively"—Erik made his voice breathy, imitating Lizbeth—"had to do a Venetian party to remind you of home."

Kevin laughed at Erik's impressive imitation, then gave the room another cursory glance. All very Italian, but... "Sorry," he said with a shrug and shake of his head, "none of this reminds me of Raleigh."

When amused, Erik's blue eyes danced. Right now, the bastards were doing the cha-cha. "That's what Kat said." He shoved his hand in his pocket and rocked back on his heels. "But Lizbeth insisted on creating an event to remind you of... and I quote... the Motherland."

The Motherland?

He tried to keep his laughter contained, but when he and Erik made eye contact, GAME OVER. After getting themselves under control and apologizing to the nearby group of grandmotherly patrons for the outburst, Kevin shifted sideways so they formed a ninety-degree angle, blocking their conversation from the others. "I've been to Italy once. I was four and I don't remember anything. And I only speak Italian because my mother made me learn."

"Which comes in handy when you don't want anyone to understand what you're saying… or when you're thinking out loud."

"True, but… Jesus… the Motherland?" He scrubbed a hand down his face and stifled another round of laughter.

"She's just trying to make you happy."

"I suppose, but if she really wanted to make me happy, we'd be in shorts and T-shirts, eating pizza and drinking beer." Which was the way he preferred to roll. Lizbeth's livelihood, however, depended on events like this, and she thrived in these environments.

He searched the room and found her working a crowd near the kitchen. Her fitted, gold gown dragged the ground and shimmered in the soft candlelight cast by a wall sconce. The halter-top was made of a combination of fabrics. The scrunched up part—ruching, she called it—was made from gold thread and beads; the other half was the same shimmery material as the skirt. Combined with her long black hair and dark eyes, she was stunning.

"This isn't all about me or Saving Grace," he said to Erik. "This is a tremendous business opportunity that also gave her a chance to test things prior to Miranda's wedding. Of course, we'll have an additional two hundred people here, and everything will take place outside. But in her mind, it was the perfect trial run."

Erik nodded thoughtfully. "I can see where that would make sense to Lizbeth."

The two fell into their own thoughts, and Kevin studied Erik's profile as he shuffled foot to foot and checked his watch, as anxious as Kevin to get this party over and done. Without much thought to taste, Kevin sipped his wine and contemplated going where the two of them had never gone before. At least not at the same time.

He wasn't sure why they'd never discussed Lizbeth or her and Erik's previous relationship. It was as if they'd come to a mutual, unspoken agreement the best thing for their friendship would be to pretend Erik hadn't had her first. Literally. After a long silence and much deliberation, Kevin decided to end the Lizbeth moratorium. "How long did you and Lizbeth date?"

Erik whipped around and his mouth fell open. He snapped the hatch shut a few times, but the thing kept flopping open into the oh-shit position.

"I understand," Kevin said. "Date isn't the best descriptor. But for the sake of this conversation and our friendship, let's go with that."

Erik nodded like a busted bobblehead and loosened his already slack tie. "Yeah, okay. That works." He tossed back the last of his wine and said, "We *saw* each other a handful of times over about six months." He lifted his shoulder nonchalantly. "Then she left for Europe and I didn't see her again until the night she showed up in Topsail, when you guys hooked up." His eyebrows dipped as he studied Kevin. "Why?"

Kevin shrugged, trying to match Erik's indifference, but doubted his friend would buy all the just-curious-and-making-conversation. "How well did you get to know her?"

Erik's eyes cut to the door a split second before his feet and body angled in the same direction.

"Not biblically, dumbass, in general." Kevin was aware standing here talking about his girlfriend—for lack of a better term—with his best friend, who once upon a time also banged said girlfriend, should leave him feeling guarded or protective, at least raging with jealousy like Erik had been over Kat.

It didn't. Digging around for any kind of emotional attachment to Lizbeth only garnered a whole lot of nothing.

And for *that*, he felt bad.

"Do you know her favorite food, favorite color, what kind of books she reads? When she stares off into space and gets a sad expression, did you figure out the cause?" At Erik's blank stare, Kevin glanced to the door and tugged at his collar again, feeling like a convict trapped in a house with the swat team closing in. He'd gotten himself into this situation, but now he had no way out and nowhere to hide. Despite his discomfort, he'd started the conversation and he needed to finish it. "How well did she get to know you?"

Erik sighed and his shoulders sagged. "I didn't bother to learn any of those things, but she didn't care about me, either. That's not what our relationship was about. We usually met out for drinks, and then…" He made a *you know* motion with his hand and cut his eyes to the wall.

A moment later, he took a deep breath, then turned to face Kevin, committing himself to the conversation despite the awkwardness. "What's going on? Why the questions after all this time?"

"I'm not sure," Kevin said, still trying to figure out the whys himself. In the past, mostly in college, Kevin and Steve, and Erik and Steve shared women. Kevin and Erik never did. Whether it was their competitive natures or an ego thing, he didn't know, but it was a well-established line they all understood would never be crossed. It seemed counterintuitive to discuss Lizbeth like this, but desperation had Kevin searching for a lifeline. "I guess I'm looking for someone else who understands her."

Erik squinted, like the increased focus would help clear things up.

Kevin squinted back to see if it worked. Nope, still confused.

"Sounds like there's trouble in paradise," Erik said, cocking his head to the side.

Kevin laugh-snorted and motioned for the guy with the drink tray to bring him another. Shitty wine was better than nothing, especially during this conversation. After snagging two glasses, he said, "We've never been in paradise, but lately…" He looked around, trying to find a nice way to explain the situation. Finally, he gave up on tact and said, "She's lost her damned mind. She's always been self-absorbed, but she's out of control."

"Yeah, she's planning a *wedding*." Erik emphasized the last word by stretching his arms wide.

"Kat didn't get like this, and it was *her* wedding."

Erik grinned. "Yeah, but our wedding was a small, intimate affair. Not one of epic proportions. And Kat didn't have a business riding on it, either."

Kat and Erik's wedding had been perfectly suited for them. "Sometimes I wonder if Miranda wouldn't have preferred something smaller, something similar to yours." He actually wondered if Miranda was ready to get married at all. She was a young twenty-two and oftentimes seemed unsettled. When he tried to talk to him about it, Wade brushed off Kevin's concerns. And Miranda accepted the proposal, so who was he to pop their balloons?

"You think Lizbeth is doing things her way, rather than Miranda's?"

"Doesn't she always?"

"You got a point." Erik stared at him as if he were studying tea leaves. "You're ready to end things."

It wasn't a question, but Kevin nodded anyway. "Yeah." The weight of his decision settled on his shoulders while simultaneously breaking something loose in his chest. His gaze traveled back to her, and he finally felt something: sadness. A soul-deep sadness because they weren't better matched, and no matter how hard he tried, they never would be.

"But?"

He turned back to Erik. "But what?"

"You know what you need to do, but something's holding you back."

"Hello…" He gave Erik a prompting look. "Wedding. No, make that *epic* wedding. Here"—he pointed to the ground—"at my house, in two weeks. If the best man dumps the maid of honor right beforehand, things will get awfully awkward and uncomfortable for everyone."

Erik opened his mouth, then closed it. Opened. Closed.

"What?"

After several tense moments of silence, Erik said, "You're too nice."

"What?" Gee, he sounded like a broken record.

"It doesn't matter who or the circumstances—your sister, your girlfriend, the homeless kid you pick up off the street and employ." At Kevin's raised brow, he said, "You gonna deny it?"

"Look how great the homeless kid turned out to be." Wade was smart and hardworking, and hiring him was one of the best decisions Kevin ever made.

Erik rolled his head around in a circle. "You're missing the point. You and Lizbeth have been on and off more than a light switch, but you still care about her. For that reason, you'll put her wants and needs before your own. Even if it makes you miserable."

Kevin glared, but it was all for show because he was having a hard time coming up with a decent argument. "So… what you're saying is I'm a pussy."

"And a dick." Erik's eyes lit up as his grin stretched wide. "Hey, check you out; you're a complete package."

"Fuck you."

"I'm just messin', trying to lighten the mood." Erik's voice was soft and cajoling, like he was trying to talk Kevin off a forty-foot ledge. He chewed at the corner of his mouth, trying to decide whether or not to continue, which was weird because Erik was usually blunt and to the point. Decision made, he said, "Kat and I are worried about you."

Kevin flinched in surprise. "Why?"

Erik rubbed his temple and took a step closer. In a low voice, barely audible over the din of the crowd, he said, "You're tense as hell and stressed all the time. SOP for me, definitely not for you." He looked at Kevin's hands. "You're drinking more and more all the time, and it seems to be getting out of hand."

Kevin's tongue stuck to roof of his mouth as heat flared under his collar. He widened his stance and squared his shoulders, going toe-to-toe and eye-to-eye with Erik. More than once they'd narrowly escaped a roll-around-in-the-dirt beat-fest, but cooler heads—as in Steve—always diffused the situation before the first punch.

Steve wasn't here tonight, however, and Kevin was carrying a ton of pent-up steam that needed venting. "Say again," he challenged.

Unimpressed with the posturing, Erik met his stare, unwavering and equally threatening. "You're double fisting piss that's being passed off as wine. You don't see the problem?"

Deep-seated anger erupted into rage as Kevin's vision turned crimson. The walls closed in around him, caging him like an animal. Cornered and isolated, exposed to the world, he wanted to come out fighting, claws exposed, going for the jugular to end the threat. He'd never wanted to live up to his nickname, Wildman, so badly.

Laughter in the distance—Kat's laughter—broke through the violent fog clouding his mind and judgment. For the second time in one day, he was forced to back the fuck off. No matter how badly he wanted to, he couldn't pummel Erik for speaking the truth.

His drinking wasn't out of control… yet. He realized, however, if he kept his current pace, it would be. He couldn't go to sleep without tossing back a few shots, and his first stop upon arriving home in the evening was always the fridge. Most nights, he drank his dinner rather than bothering to fix something of substance, so… yeah… there might be an issue.

Erik relaxed and took a step back, easing off his aggression in direct proportion to Kevin stepping off his. "Is it the job? Lizbeth? The wedding? Hell, all of the above?" The stress lines around his eyes smoothed and his gaze turned imploring. "What can we do to help?"

"Nothing," Kevin said, setting the glasses on the side table so the tremble in his hand wasn't obvious. He pushed his fingers through his hair and blew out a breath. "Work has been a bitch." And that was before things blew up over the water tower. And, as much as he hated to admit it, he added, "Lizbeth is definitely part of the problem."

"What are you going to do?"

He threw both hands into the air, palms up. "What can I do right now? I mean, look around." He made a wide sweeping gesture with his arms. "She threw a party to remind me of 'the Motherland.'" He laughed, then sobered. "Seriously, though, how can I do anything this close to her sister's wedding? She's been planning for a year, and she's already self-conscious about her baby sister getting married first." He shook his head. "Forget Lizbeth. I can't do that to Wade and Miranda. Things would be so awkward and tense between us. I'm afraid their day would be ruined by stress and Lizbeth's dramatics."

Erik pressed his lips together and gave Kevin a sympathetic look. "I'm sorry, bro. You're definitely wedged into a tight spot." He glanced to Lizbeth, then back to Kevin. "I guess you've stuck it out this long. Another few weeks won't kill ya. Right?"

Kevin yanked at the tie, which seemed even tighter than ten minutes before. "That's what I keep telling myself. But if I have to keep wearing these damned ties, I'm not so sure."

Chapter Four

Two hours later, right on Kevin's optimistic schedule, the house emptied, leaving only Erik, Kat, and Janelle Gentry, the executive director of Saving Grace. Another hour later, most everything had been cleaned up and put away, and they'd gotten an official accounting of the evening's fundraising efforts. In addition to volunteering at the shelter on a weekly basis, Kat had taken on the unofficial role of fundraiser, and she and Janelle were thrilled with the evening's response.

"You gonna be around this weekend?" Erik asked Kevin, pushing the side door open for Kat while Lizbeth showed Janelle out the front.

"Nah, I gotta be in Myrtle Beach first thing in the morning. I promised Marianne I'd keep Spencer so she can run some errands and have lunch with a friend."

"Why don't you bring him back here?" Lizbeth said, smiling sweetly as she stepped into the kitchen.

The hair on Kevin's neck shot to attention, prickles of alarm danced up his arm, and a neon sign flashed in his mind. *BEWARE!*

Lizbeth excelled at being bold, extra-spicy, sometimes sour—never sweet.

"I haven't been around kids since Miranda was little," she said when he continued to stare. She cut her eyes to the side and dipped her chin—another major fail, because she sucked even worse at being coy.

"I need the practice."

All this Shirley Temple-ing, in conjunction with the topic of kids, would cause most men to panic as they envisioned their future circling the drain. He didn't understand her motives, but he was positive she wasn't telling him in some off-handed, roundabout way she was pregnant.

If that *was* her intent, she had the wrong man.

Even though she'd been on the pill when they first hooked up, and as far as he knew still was, he *always* used a condom to ensure this type of thing never happened. He wanted kids. He wanted a houseful of kids. Just not right now and certainly not with Lizbeth.

Erik, obviously not privy to that information, hit the panic button on Kevin's behalf. Sweat beaded on his upper lip, and rather than dancing, his wide eyes wailed a stanza of "Taps."

Kevin made a sudden move to snag Erik's attention, then shook his head and smiled, reassuring his friend, Lizbeth didn't just drop a massive pregnancy bomb.

Kat, standing outside, blissfully unaware of the holy-shit-what's-Lizbeth-talking-about taking place on the inside, yelled into the house, "Give me another two months and you can have all the practice you want."

Erik grinned at his wife like a man who hit the lottery, then swung back around to Lizbeth. The smile vanished, and he cut a worried glance at Kevin. "Call me," he said. "We need to talk."

He tucked Kat's hand in his and led her across the expansive lawn running between their houses. When Erik first approached Kevin and Steve about buying the chunk of land along the Pamlico River, Kevin shut him down. Being from Raleigh, with most of his jobs in Myrtle Beach, he didn't need another house to deal with. Steve and Erik kept at him and eventually wore him down. Even though it was a pain in the ass to drive back and forth, he was glad he caved. Most of the time, it offered a respite from the demands of his job, and he wished he had more time to spend here.

When Kat and Erik disappeared from view, he cut off the outside lights and stripped his tie off so fast he nearly ripped it. He tossed it onto the chair with his discarded jacket and beelined for the fridge. Erik's concerned voice of reason whispered in his ear, but his selective hearing knocked the noisy bastard out with a one-two combination.

Even a non-drinker would toss back a few after a day like this, so he refused to feel guilty for spending a little quality time with Bud and Jack.

"Will you bring Spencer here for the weekend?" Lizbeth asked.

"No." He winced as the response came out harsher than he intended. "I only have him tomorrow, not all weekend."

"So?"

After a long, refreshing pull of his ice-cold beer, he said, "So? I'm not dragging him up here for one day."

"You drive back and forth all the time." Her husky voice disintegrated to a nasally whine.

"I have to for work, and I don't enjoy it." He tried Erik's squint-for-increased-focus move as he worked to decipher her sudden interest in Spencer. "No six-year-old wants to spend nearly seven hours in the car only to hang out someplace for two hours." He chuckled as he imagined his precocious nephew crossing his arms and rolling his brown eyes behind his round, wire-frame glasses. The word of the day: lame.

"But I want to see him."

Kevin took a step back and crossed his arms and ankles as he leaned against the counter. "Why?"

She glanced away and extinguished the candles on the counter, then went to work stacking plates… the same ones Kat had taken out of the dishwasher and stacked moments earlier. "He's an important part of your life. I want to get to know him better."

He drank his beer and watched the tendrils of smoke drift into the air before slowly evaporating. Spencer had been an important part of his life from his first breath. Hell, from the moment Kevin found out his unwed baby sister would make him an uncle, he made the baby a priority. Spencer was four when Lizbeth entered the picture, so why the sudden interest? How had Spencer become a pawn on her chessboard?

"I'll tell you what," he said, dumping his empty bottle into the recycling bin before going to the fridge for another. "You can come to Myrtle Beach with me and stay the weekend. I'll bring you back sometime Monday. Or, you can drive separately and come back whenever you want."

She abandoned the dishes in favor of freeing a few buttons on his dress shirt. "Maybe." Translation: *No, thank you. I'll just get what I want by manipulating you through sex.*

He tightened his grip on the bottle and squeezed his eyes shut as she kissed the center of his neck, then nibbled her way up to his ear.

"Lizbeth, I'm not going to change my mind. In addition to Spencer, I left Wade dealing with a problem—"

"Do you really want to talk shop right now?" She licked the shell of his ear and released the remaining buttons, then tugged his shirt out of his pants. Running her hands along his sides and around to his back, she whispered, "Or would you rather do something else? Like me."

He knew her plan, could see the blueprint laid out before him. He wanted to tell her he wasn't interested in sex tonight, especially not when she used it as a method of manipulation, but when she bit down on his bottom lip, the sharp sting was like pulling the pin from a grenade.

She tried to stroke her tongue over his lip, to soothe the pain. But he jerked his head away and allowed the pain to ignite a series of blasting caps along his central nervous system.

How ironic he hadn't been able to draw forth any emotion before, because now, every negative emotion a man could feel swirled in his gut like a Molotov cocktail waiting for a light. When she nipped at his collarbone and pinched his nipple between her finger and thumb, the charge detonated.

On instinct, he wrapped his hand around the back of her head, angled his mouth over hers, and took her with angry force.

In the back of his mind, he knew continuing to sell his soul to the devil would only get him in deeper. But the devil drove a hard bargain, reminding him they were, technically, still involved. What did it matter if this short-term want was at odds with his long-term needs? Why not have sex to work off a shitty day?

A flash of an image pressed at the edge of his mind, causing him to break the kiss and step back. He opened his eyes and stared at Lizbeth's dark hair, shaking off the memory of a long, blond braid. The building inspector had taunted him all evening, but he was drawing the line here. She wasn't invited to this particular party.

Lizbeth's eyes filled with questions as she studied his face. Sensing his retreat, she hastily unbuckled his belt, unbuttoned his pants, and slipped her hand inside his boxers. His breath lodged in his throat and his eyes crossed as she grabbed his erection and squeezed.

Fuck yeah.

His head dropped back on his shoulders and a hiss pushed through his lips as she pressed her mouth to his chest and ran her tongue over his nipple.

"Are we doing this here, on the kitchen table?" Lizbeth purred. "Or are you taking me to a proper bed?"

His cock jerked in response, anxious to get on with things, regardless of the location. Given the extent of pent-up energy he needed to expel, this would to take a while. The kitchen table, while hot and accommodating under the right circumstances, would eventually become uncomfortable. Switching positions was fine; stopping to change locations wasn't.

In a voice roughened by sexual desire and self-recrimination, he said, "Bed. Now."

After tucking Michy into bed, Sam spent the next fifteen minutes scanning channels with the remote. Nothing captured, let alone held, her attention, so she grabbed a fresh beer, her pen and notepad, and broke out the Vanguard Subdivision file—the reason she was late picking up Michy.

She'd been in her car, pulling out of the lot, when she decided to go back and grab the Vanguard files. Experience proved options were limited in cases like this, but she did have practice, as well as the hardheaded resolve to figure out a reasonable solution.

An hour and a half later, she had several scenarios mapped out for Mazze and Wade to discuss at their Monday morning breakfast. She noted what she could do to move the process along, and even though it wasn't much, cutting off a week was better than standing still.

She gave the TV one last chance, but after another disappointing round of five-hundred-and-nothing, she chucked the remote and went to bed.

Alone in the dark, she contemplated the paradox of craving daytime solitude while dreading the quiet at night. Being home alone during the day, while Michy was at daycare, seemed naughty and taboo, and she cherished every minute of the tranquility. Home alone in the evening, lying on the couch, watching TV or reading, was plain lonely.

Crawling into a cold, empty bed was hell.

She reached for one of the flannel-covered pillows she kept as a snuggle buddy and tucked it close to her side. Even though the covering was warm, the pillow didn't ruffle her hair while breathing, nor did it return the hug.

From the nightstand, she picked up the business card she'd found in her pocket while undressing. She stroked her fingers over the raised print, tracing the numbers of Mazze's cell phone, and wondered, again, how he spent his Friday nights?

He said he'd be in Riverside tonight, but did he have a local hangout where he normally spent his evenings? If she ever went out, might she run into him?

Did he drink, and if yes, did he prefer whiskey or beer? Would the taste linger on his lips, acting as fuel to her fire when they kissed?

She closed her eyes and pictured his full bottom lip, so damned tempting and perfect for sucking and tasting.

And, Lord, his eyes… When he hovered over her, taking her, would they be hot and hungry, or soften with tenderness?

What kind of lover would he be?

She laughed into the dark, cavernous room.

He emitted a powerful, raw magnetism and moved with such a confident prowess, she knew he'd be amazing.

Her nipples hardened as she imagined him touching… teasing… stroking… pleasing.

She deflated into the mattress as Michael's words pushed through the barrier of her subconscious. She closed her eyes and gripped the pillow close to her chest, trying to stifle the expanding ache that always accompanied the memory. Still reeling from her father's sudden death, his words cut so deeply, the only way to survive had been to shut down.

As weeks turned into months, the numbness gave way to overwhelming grief, and she plummeted to the bottom of an emotional well. She spent countless days rehashing the night she walked into his office and found his secretary bent over his desk, him fucking her from behind, the picture of Sam and Michaela staring her in the face. Given everything, it was odd to think about, but Sam wondered a million times if he or Sheila even noticed the picture.

His only explanation for the affair had been those cutting, parting words. *You're ice, Sam. Of course I found someone else. Why wouldn't I find a* real *woman?* She'd always been self-conscious about her lack of femininity, so his words served as miniature shotgun blasts, ripping her apart, leaving her barely breathing.

Cheri, and her not-so-gentle reminder that Sam needed to get a grip for Michaela's sake, had been a lifeline, dragging her out of the dark, desolate hole. Cheri worked Sam for months, but finally convinced her to make a fresh start—away from the overwhelming reminders of all she'd lost with her dad's passing, away from Michael and his constant torment, and especially away from her traitorous brothers.

The decision was terrifying, but Cheri had been right. She was going nowhere fast in Columbia, and in Myrtle Beach, she'd at least have a chance of finding peace and happiness.

Here she was, two months later. For the most part, she'd learned her way around Horry County and no longer needed the GPS to guide her every turn. She'd gotten used to their new house and didn't jerk awake in the middle of the night, trying to figure out where she was. She and Michaela were still adjusting to not having family nearby, but they were doing okay.

At what point, she wondered, would she get used to sleeping alone?

She flipped her eyes open and stared at the bottom dresser drawer—

the one holding more toys and lubes and gadgets and gizmos than the world's best-stocked sex shop. Cheri was an in-home adult toy party consultant, and anytime they came out with a new product, Sam was first in line to buy.

All for the sake of giving Cheri an honest customer review, of course.

The truth was, even though Michael thought she was icy and uninterested in sex, he couldn't have been more wrong. After Michaela was born, the stress of having a newborn in the house caused things to become strained between them. Just as things were getting back on track, her dad died, and her world collapsed.

She needed to be loved and cuddled, held close and reassured everything would be all right. All he wanted was to rut, have a quick orgasm without regard to her, then roll over and go to sleep.

It wasn't that she didn't like sex. She did. A lot. She just no longer wanted to have sex with him.

She slipped out of bed, sank to her knees, and opened the drawer. So many choices… so little enthusiasm. Some nights, she had a strong desire to go through the drawer and experiment with everything. She enjoyed learning her body, figuring out what excited her and what didn't… which, turns out, there wasn't much she didn't enjoy.

Tonight, however, Friday-night fatigue made this more a function of need than playful, experimental fun. She picked up the Waskly Wabbit and studied the thick, vibrating shaft and tiny flicking ears. Normally a crowd favorite, tonight the little fella held no appeal. She tossed him back into the drawer and hesitated as her hand drifted across the spanking strap. She fingered the rough leather before moving on to the wooden paddle.

Sitting up on her knees, she gave herself a few smacks across the ass and hissed as the sting spread down to her thighs. She loved the pleasurable pain that came from being spanked—which had been a complete shock—but playing with the strap and paddle drove home the solitude more than anything else.

She replaced the paddle and picked up the Double Dare—a good time with not one, but two imaginary studs. She'd had serious reservations about ordering the intimidating double vibrator and doubted she'd ever use it. After polishing off a six-pack one night, she decided to take the double dong for a spin. Surprisingly, it became her favorite.

She gave a heartless laugh. Who would've thought the Ice Queen would enjoy a pretend threesome? However, she needed to be in an adventurous frame of mind and willing to expend a ton of energy slipping into a deep enough headspace to buy the fantasy. She wasn't up for that much exertion tonight, so she dropped it back into the drawer and, after another cursory glance through the stash, grabbed the basic, no-frills Long Dong.

She stripped off her nightshirt as she crawled into bed, turned the vibrator on, and closed her eyes. Several moments of strategically placed flicks and rubs barely had her motor running. But after two minutes of thinking about Kevin Mazze's dark eyes, dark hair, strong jawline, and full lips, she was on fire.

She slid the vibrating tip through the slick folds of her sex, then brushed it over her clit. With her eyes closed and her mind focused on Mazze, she imagined him filling her as she slowly drove it inside.

She arched her back, lifting her breasts toward his waiting mouth… only to find empty space above and hollowness within. With no other option than to take matters into her own hands, she massaged her breast, then clamped down on the nipple. The pinch revved her up, but not nearly like it would've coming from his large, work-roughened hand.

She plunged the vibrator deeper, moaning as it rubbed against her

G-spot. Would Kevin know where to find the magic button? How long before he had her spinning out of control?

Images of his dark eyes, filled with ravenous heat, swam through her mind as she built the fantasy: his large arms wrapped around her, his weight forcing her into the mattress as he drove deep.

She cranked up the volume and worked the vibrator over her G-spot, then pinched her clit, going for the kill. She arched her back and bucked against the pulsing of the vibrator as the orgasm built momentum and consumed her from the inside out.

As always, the unassisted orgasm ended too soon and left her void of any kind of post-orgasmic bliss.

After allowing her heart rate to settle and her legs to regain their density, she climbed out of bed, used the bathroom, and stashed the cleaned toy away in the safety of the drawer.

The sheets were damp and colder than before.

Just like her soul.

She never wanted another husband, but she needed a sex partner, someone to share her bed, even if only occasionally.

Michael had been wrong about her not liking sex, so maybe he was wrong about her being a real woman, too. Men often looked at her as she walked down the street or beach. There must be something they found attractive. Something about her had attracted Michael in the first place.

She'd never pursued a man before, but desperate times called for desperate measures. She swept her hand across the bed and found the crushed business card, forgotten in the heat of the moment. Her chances might be those of the proverbial snowball, but she never backed down from a challenge, especially from something she really wanted.

She couldn't remember ever wanting anything as much as she wanted Kevin Mazze.

What should've been a satisfying ending to a long and arduous day only added another layer of shit to Kevin's mile-high dung pile.

He'd taken Lizbeth three different times in three different ways, leaving her exhausted but content, sleeping peacefully in his bed, while he sat in the chair, hollow as a straw—with the exception of the five beers he knocked back—searching for something, anything, to fill the void.

Tonight's fucking had been hard and fast, probably brutal if anyone were unfortunate enough to play witness. No Mr. Nice Guy in this bedroom. He'd carried enough aggression to start a war, but she spurred him on, needing to be taken even harder.

The sex had never been sweet or gentle, but rather edgy, almost angry at times. Over the past few months, the ferocity increased.

Everything about their relationship was destructive. And the worst part? Neither seemed to care.

Erik wanted to know the cause of Kevin's drinking. This was the root of it all.

After the moaning and groaning and coming was over, he always needed something to wash away the disgust and self-loathing that crept in on the heels of the post-coital exhaustion.

Worse yet was the reason he stuck with Lizbeth in the first place. Watching Kat and Erik build their life together gradually ate him alive from the inside out. Not because he wanted Kat for himself or because of jealousy. He was so damned happy for his friend that lately, aside from Spencer, Erik's joy was the only bright spot in Kevin's life.

But Kevin had come to realize he wanted the same thing for himself. The Wildman, who swore to never settle down with one woman, wanted to be tamed.

He'd known all along Lizbeth wouldn't be a permanent fixture in his life, but having someone temporarily beat being alone. At least that's what he told himself before Lizbeth went crazy. By the time he reached his breaking point, the wedding had closed in, and he found himself trapped.

His gaze dropped to her high-heeled shoe and, not for the first time, the damned thing morphed into a ratty work boot.

Since crawling out of bed to drink in earnest, Samantha Wallace dominated his thoughts, which only intensified his mental anguish.

She fascinated him on every level, from her rocking body to the history behind her boots to her mysterious eye color—an unknown that was driving him batshit crazy. He didn't have room for another complication, however. His plate was already loaded with Lizbeth, the wedding, and now the Vanguard problem.

Oh… and apparently, he also had a drinking problem, so throw that shit on top and call it gravy.

The only way to keep from joining Lizbeth on the crazy train would be to avoid women altogether. If he stayed in Myrtle Beach, away from Lizbeth, he wouldn't have to worry about repeating tonight's performance. He'd need to deal with Samantha from time to time, but she had no idea how much she attracted him. He could keep things professional until he had the wedding behind him and ended things with Lizbeth. Then, after he got himself under control, he would pursue her and see if anything developed.

Until then… celibacy was the name of the game.

Chapter Five

$\mathcal{M}$yrtle Beach's Boardwalk, a mishmash of activities and shopping, offered something for everyone. Along with the Ferris wheel, there were several rides available for adrenaline junkies, one being a giant slingshot that launched riders into the stratosphere… Okay, so it only sent the passenger sixty feet in the air… but still.

For the less adventurous, who preferred spectator sports to thrill rides, a jumbotron at the edge of the pavilion played popular afternoon sporting events. And for the truly sluggish, there were lots of bars and cafes scattered about, where one could eat and drink until their little hearts grew merry.

As far as Sam was concerned, the best thing about the Boardwalk was the world-famous, massively messy, awesomely unhealthy but so friggin' fantastic foot-long chilidog.

The promenade wasn't nearly as crowded as a few weeks before, but Sam still doubted they'd be able to find one six-year-old boy—assuming he was at the Boardwalk and not wandering around on the beach, or at a different location altogether.

Sitting on a bench in the middle of the pavilion, she handed Michaela her hot dog and drink and spread the fries between them. After making sure Michy was settled, she closed her eyes and bit into the gooey mess. The bread nestled her lips like a fluffy pillow as flavors exploded on her tongue—ketchup, tangy mustard, sweet relish, spicy chili—

Her moment of nirvana came to a crashing halt when Michaela yelled, "Mommy, Mommy, Mommy. There's Spencer." Sam opened her eyes to find her daughter pointing across the crowd to the small seawall separating the pavilion from the sand. "I told you we'd find him. I knew it." Michy waved her arms like she was trying to take flight and yelled, "Spencer, Spencer!"

Everyone in the area turned to them… everyone except Spencer, apparently, and panic quickly ensued.

When another massive wail failed to catch his attention, Michy scrambled down from her perch, dropped her hot dog and drink onto the bench, and took off. She vaulted over the concrete barricade like a professional hurdler and sprinted down the beach like an escaped convict.

"Shit." Sam dropped her hot dog onto the paper wrapper, grabbed her bag, and bolted after her.

She jostled around a toddler chasing a sea gull, then hit the sand "sidewalk" in pursuit. In the blink of an eye, she went from running to flying to diving face first into the sand.

Blinding, white-hot pain shot through her ankle and up her leg. "Son of a fucking bitch!" She rolled onto her back, brought her knee to her chest, and wrapped her arms around her leg, gasping for air.

The pain was so intense, she couldn't pinpoint where it originated, maybe the ankle. Despite the horrendous throbbing, her daughter was still scurrying down the beach, and somehow, someway, she had to get to her feet.

She pushed to her knees, preparing to go vertical, when Michy's sweet voice rang out. "Mommy!" The concerned cry was the most beautiful sound she ever heard.

Thank you, Jesus.

She didn't have to run anywhere. She didn't even have to walk, because her baby bird returned. Sam flopped onto her back, squeezed her eyes closed to stop the sting, and bit down on her lip to squelch the quivering.

"This is going to hurt, but we have to get your shoe off. Your foot is already swelling."

Her breath left in a whoosh and she forgot to take another as the deep… vaguely familiar voice registered. She cracked her eye open and, for the briefest moment, wondered if she'd died and gone to heaven where all the angels looked like Kevin Mazze.

He shoved his sunglasses onto the top of his head, giving her a good look at his red and watery eyes with dark half moons below and a two day-old shadow coloring his jaw. This was no angel, and wherever he'd been last night, he obviously had a devil of a time.

"I'm sorry," he said, flinching as he unbuckled her sandal and slipped it off her foot.

Agony ripped through her leg, all the way to her stomach, erasing any fantasy she had of being dead or in the presence of angels. "Ooww… Son of a"—Sam glanced at her daughter—"beach! Sheet, that hurts."

"Keep breathing. Take long… deep breaths." His low tone and slow cadence compelled her to do as he said. "Good. Keep going. Deep breath in, slow exhale."

After a few more Lamaze-type breaths, the pain morphed from a concentrated oh-holy-fuck-that-hurts into a body-wide throb.

"Spencer, come here." Kevin reached into his back pocket for his wallet and pulled out a five.

Despite the nausea rolling northward and the burning desire to curl into a fetal position and cry for her mommy, Sam focused on Kevin Mazze's face, then on Spencer… from afterschool… who had the same dark hair and compelling midnight eyes as Kevin.

She gasped. "Spencer's yours?"

Kevin ignored her question and spoke to Spencer. "Give that to Miss Amy at the snow cone booth and tell her we need a baggie full of ice and one of her dish rags. I'm going to get Samantha up to the pavilion."

Spencer ran off to parts unknown with Michy on his heels. Sam tried to sit up in protest, but Kevin pressed a hand to her shoulder and shook his head. "I can see the booth from here. They're fine. Let's get your foot elevated to minimize the swelling."

He laid her sandal across her stomach, slid his arms under her back and knees, and scooped her up in one fluid motion. "That was a hell of a fall," he said, while using his foot to push sand into the hole she'd fallen into. "Anything besides your ankle hurt?"

Sam was as overwhelmed and vulnerable as if she'd been parked naked in the middle of Main Street during the Labor Day parade. Her foot was on fire, but she'd survive the injury.

She may, however, die from mortification.

Sand stuck to her sweaty skin and itched so bad she wanted to scratch like a dog with fleas. Her daddy used to say, *"Grit is good for the craw,"* and though she never understood the meaning, she hoped the saying was true, because hell would freeze over before she'd embarrass herself further by spitting out the sand stuck between her teeth.

Adding to the trauma, Kevin—her fantasy man—not only witnessed her swan dive, but felt the need to come to her rescue.

Memories from the night before rushed her, and even though he didn't know he'd been her dream lover, she panicked. "I'm fine. Put me down. Put me down."

"What the hell? Stop fighting me." His words were like a cracking whip, instantly stifling her wild attempt to break free. "Does anything else hurt?"

She shook her head in short, jerky motions. "Only my pride. I'm fine. You can put me down now." When he kept walking toward the pavilion, she said, "Really. Any time now."

A breathtaking smile lit his face and laughter vibrated from his chest into her side. "You are feisty, aren't you?"

"Yeah," she admitted. "But usually with more finesse."

Of all the ways she imagined launching a campaign to attract and seduce, none included falling flat on her face. She wrapped her arms around his neck to hold on and ducked her head to keep from hiding behind her hands.

The pain was still incredible, but cradled against his body with her arms around his neck, breathing in his earthy scent, she was shocked to find heat of a different kind blooming. Never one to pass up an opportunity, she gave in to the temptation tickling her fingers and sifted them through the curls at the base of his skull.

His body tensed, and he stopped breathing. The response initially made her think the subtle advance was unwelcome and she quickly let go of the silky strands. But then his arms tightened, pulling her closer to his chest. His reaction wasn't obvious, but enough to let her know he wasn't repulsed by her touch.

She lifted her gaze to his, hoping for a clearer indication of his thoughts. But rather than being warm and inviting, his eyes narrowed as he stared at her sunglasses. As they bounced from one lens to the other, his jaw flexed and frown lines creased around the edges of his lips and eyes. Not the reaction she hoped for. His mixed signals made her feel awkward and left her with that naked on Main Street feeling again.

She wasn't petite, but she didn't weigh a ton, either. Certainly not enough for someone in excellent condition to be overexerting himself. The day was warm, but not a scorcher… so what was up with the bead of sweat trickling down his long sideburn.

He swallowed a few times in rapid succession, and his voice was a little rougher than normal when he said, "Let's find a place in the shade to sit while we ice your ankle. Because of the swelling, I don't think X-rays will show anything right now, but I can take you to urgent care, if you like."

"Thanks, but that's not necessary." She pointed to the bench she and Michaela vacated moments earlier. "Look, my awesome-dog's still there."

Kevin grinned. "Ah, that explains it." At her frown, he added, "I wondered about the mustard on your nose."

A fresh wave of humiliation shot through her. She swiped at her nose and sure as shit, her fingers came away with a streak of yellow. "Jesus, can this day get any more embarrassing?"

"Did you shit your pants when you fell?"

She gasped in shock. "What? No!"

Kevin laughed and eased her onto the bench. "There ya go. It could've been worse."

Despite the circumstances, she laughed. She always considered laughter the best medicine, and before she could gain control, the small chuckle turned into near hysterics.

"Miss Amy said come back and get more if we need to," Spencer said, handing him two big bags of slushy ice, a couple of towels, and Kevin's five-dollar bill.

"Thanks, squirt. You did good."

"Mommy, are you okay? You scared me when you screamed."

Sam wrapped her arms around Michy in a reassuring hug. "I'm fine, sweetie. It's just a little owie that'll be better in no time. And, for the record, I didn't scream."

Michy giggled and Kevin grinned. "Yes, you did, and it was loud, too."

"Great." Sam sighed and rolled her eyes to Kevin. "The other thing you asked about... Apparently, it's the only thing I didn't do."

She'd fallen, screamed, nearly cried, had mustard on her nose, sand on her skin, grit in her teeth, and an ankle the size of a basketball—all in front of the sexiest man she'd ever met, the man she fantasized about the night before... the man she hoped to seduce.

Despite her shortcomings and the accompanying drama, he was still here, using a feather-light touch to drape the towel over her ankle and foot, and readying the ice. He didn't drop the bag in place, but instead, let it hover for a moment, giving her time to adjust to the weight and sensation of the cold before settling it in place.

"We'll leave that on for about thirty minutes, then figure out where to go from there."

Sam didn't do well being nursed, and she hated to disrupt Kevin and Spencer's afternoon. And a little privacy to spit and scratch would be awesome.

"Thank you for your help, but I'll be fine. There's no need for you and Spencer to hang around here. I don't know how much time you get to spend with him, so please"—she shooed him away like a stray—"go do whatever you had planned."

He leaned against the wooden pillar behind him and crossed his arms. "Spencer's my nephew, and I have him all the time." He said the last few words in a heavy, dragged-out nature, like being with his nephew was a major burden, but the grin on his face and the warmth in his eyes said otherwise.

Michaela and Spencer, with their beautiful five and six-year-old tendencies, had gotten on with the business of having fun and were playing in the sand by the seawall.

Unable to spit, Sam sipped from the straw in her cup and swished the soda around in her mouth. She eyed the chilidog, considering another bite… or twelve. But at the rate she was going, she'd end up choking and need Kevin to do the Heimlich. She rested her hands on the bench behind her and leaned back, while Kevin carefully shifted the bag.

"So, it's true," she said through gritted teeth, trying to ignore the micro-bursts of fire accompanying each shift of the ice.

"What's true?"

"You really are a nice guy."

He grimaced. "So I've been told."

She smiled at his discomfort. "You're humble, too. I heard lots of good things about you, but… somehow, I missed those qualities yesterday."

He laughed and ran a thumb across his brow. "Yeah, sorry. Yesterday wasn't one of my finer moments."

"I understand. That's why I—" The discomfort of the ice pushed beyond her tolerance level, cutting off her thought and causing her foot to jerk. "Holy sh—" She snapped her mouth shut and glanced to the seawall, making sure her pint-sized police officer hadn't caught the near slip. She blew out a breath and let the pain radiate outward, then dissipate.

She hated to make Michy leave, but she couldn't keep an eye on her with this ankle. Scratch that. She could keep an eye on her, but that's all. If Michy got in trouble in the water, Sam would be at the mercy of the lifeguard and strangers. Should a stranger decide to snap up her little cutie pie, Sam would be helpless.

Chalk up another Mommy Fail of the Year nomination. At this rate, she'd have such a huge advantage on any other candidates, she'd have the award wrapped up by the end of the weekend.

She cut her eyes to Mazze, who watched her way too closely. Given the circumstances, it seemed odd to enjoy his company, but her pleasure wasn't important. One disappointed child was more than enough, so she gave another go at getting him to move along.

"There's no need to hang out here," she said. "I've already interrupted your day enough."

He cocked his head to the side and grinned. "Trying to get rid of me?"

As he reached for the ice again, she grabbed his wrist to stop him. They both froze and stared at the connection.

Breaking the trance, she said, "Yes, because if you keep touching that bag, I'm going to flag down the police and charge you with assault."

His laughter rose all the way to his eyes, which seemed to be clearing, and rather than settling back into a frown, his mouth maintained the smile. He delicately lifted the ice from her foot, giving her a moment of relief.

"We didn't have any special plans," he said, distracting her with conversation as he slowly lowered the quickly melting slush back into place. He watched her face for signs of distress, and when satisfied she was okay, he let go. "To be honest, I hadn't planned on staying long. We were going to get a snow cone and then head back to the house so he can swim while I sit in the shade and drink cold beer."

Sam's facial muscles slackened and she imagined her eyes turning glassy. "That sounds like a great plan. Why'd you even bother coming here?"

He nodded to the kids. "Spencer said his friend Michaela would be here and insisted on stopping."

"I've only met him a few times, but he seems as precocious as Michy. I've been meaning to talk to Marianne to see about arranging some play dates, but I keep missing her at afterschool."

A few play dates with Uncle Kevin would also be awesome.

Yesterday, all worked up and aggressive, he appealed to her wilder side, making her wonder how rough and rowdy he might be in the sack. Today, kicked back and relaxed, tenderly lifting the ice pack from her ankle when he thought it might be too much, then gently replacing it, she had a whole different set of images of what sex with him might be like.

As he repositioned the ice bag again, his shoulder rolled under the plain white T-shirt, his bicep flexed and relaxed, and his eyes narrowed in concentration. His chest stopped moving and his gaze snapped to her face, making sure she was okay as he slowly released the bag.

"I have an idea."

She'd been so lost in thought—taking in every detail of his body—his idea was probably for her to stop ogling.

Heat crept into her face and she pressed the drink cup to the back of her neck, pretending the temperature had gotten to be too much. "What's that?"

"You and Michaela come back to my place. The kids can play. You can prop your foot up and relax, and I'll play cabana boy, bringing you cold drinks and fresh ice packs as needed." He smiled and spread his arms wide. "How can you possibly refuse that invitation?"

She laughed and sighed. *How, indeed?*

Normally fiercely independent, she realized her ankle would be a problem, and an extra set of hands might be nice. Michy wouldn't have her afternoon ruined, Spencer would have a playmate, which was always more fun than playing alone, and Sam would have time with cabana-boy Mazze.

She gripped the cup with both hands to keep from fanning herself. "Are you sure?"

He glanced at the rolling ocean and rubbed the back of his neck. Turning back to her, he smiled and said, "Yeah, I'm positive. Spencer and I will enjoy the company."

Chapter Six

*A*s Kevin pulled out of the parking lot, he checked the rearview mirror to make sure Sam followed, then headed toward Grissom Parkway. Since she drove a stick shift, it was impossible for her to drive her truck and push the clutch with the sprained ankle. His truck was an automatic, so they put both booster seats in her truck, and he handled the manual transmission and the kids.

All she had to worry about was guarding her foot and following him through traffic. All he had to worry about was not losing the rest of his damned mind.

Stay away from women—the grand plan he formulated early this morning. Now, here he was, taking Samantha home... his home, no less.

But what could he do? He couldn't just leave her there, dealing with an injury and a five-year-old all on her own. And it was a good thing he insisted she come with him; otherwise, she would've ended up driving her truck home and probably doing further damage to her ankle.

The kids were having a great time, giggling and playing and chattering away in a language only they understood. They seemed to have developed their own version of pig Latin... or maybe it was excited kid speak. Either way, it wasn't English or Italian and he *non capiva*.

He checked the mirror and smiled at the blond hair and mirrored shades peering above his steering wheel. Samantha Wallace was tough as steel, and so was the little girl sitting in the seat behind him. When she heard her mamma scream and turned to see her fall, her look of terror and the wave of angst rushing from her tiny body nearly crippled him. As Sam writhed in pain with her teeth clamped down on her lip, Michaela fisted her hands at her side and mimicked her mamma perfectly.

Both would've felt better if they'd let the tears go, but he had to respect their grit and determination to lock down their physical and emotional pain and deal with it in their own way. Neither would've appreciated being coddled, so he shut down his Mr. Fix-it tendencies and his desire to nurture and met their needs with as much emotional aloofness and cool sympathy as he could muster.

After being in constant demand, Mr. Fix-it still reeled from being shoved to the side, unwanted.

He chuckled as he slid to the left, giving himself room to change gears on the Toyota four-by-four. He should've guessed her personal vehicle wouldn't be a car. A truck was definitely more her style… a little one was perfect.

Man, rough sex with her would be complicated. He'd always be afraid of breaking her.

Wait… What? Rough sex?

Where the hell did that thought come from? Yeah, he thought she was hot. Yes, he was attracted to her on every level. Yes, he enjoyed rough sex sometimes. But why was he thinking about rough sex with the pixie… right now?

Because that's where his subconscious mind had been parked and idling since she got up in his face and questioned his hearing.

He took a deep breath and shut down the raunchy thoughts revving his body into high gear, eager to turn thought into reality. For the next two weeks, or as long as he was involved with Lizbeth, Samantha

Wallace was off-limits. A professional relationship, like he had with Wade or any of the other builders in the area, was fine. Anything more… was not. He was a strong-willed man; he could do this.

Besides, he wanted a new type of relationship, one based on more than great sex. He wanted someone he could talk to, about work, about fun stuff, about a dumb movie, or about nothing in particular. He wanted someone who would enjoy spending time in Riverside. Someone laidback and fun, like Kat and Erik and Steve. Someone who would become his entire world.

He had no idea if Samantha Wallace might be that person, but in order to get what he wanted, he needed to go about things differently. No more convenient lays and one-nighters. He needed to take things slow, lay the groundwork, build a solid foundation, and *then* take things to the physical.

He checked his rearview again, making sure Samantha was still with him, then turned into the neighborhood he called home these days. He stopped at the guard shack and waved to Lamar, the daytime security guard.

"You got yourself a new whip," Lamar said, ambling over. He bent down to look into the truck and broke into a toothy grin. "And a new kid."

Kevin threw his thumb over his shoulder, pointing to Sam who sat in his truck behind him. "A friend of mine hurt her foot, so she can't drive a clutch. This is her daughter, Michaela."

Hearing her name, Michaela peeked around the back of the seat and saw Lamar. Her blue eyes widened as she took in the patches on Lamar's uniform and her mouth dropped open. "What'd you do wrong?" she whispered.

Nothing yet, Kevin thought. "He's the guard that works here and makes sure no one comes into the neighborhood who doesn't belong."

She looked around at the gated entrance, then peered through the windshield into the neighborhood. "Holy cow. You live here? In a castle?"

"Not exactly."

Lamar rapped his knuckles on the bed of the truck. "Have a great day, Mr. Ma—" Catching himself, he cleared his throat and said, "Mr. Kevin."

"Thanks, Lamar. You too." He pulled through the gate and watched Lamar check Samantha over as he waved her past.

Once she passed by, Lamar's grin was light-bulb bright as he gave a thumbs-up for Kevin to see in his mirror. Kevin waved out the window to show his agreement, then followed the winding road around to the Holden mansion, his temporary home away from home.

He pulled to the side of the garage and motioned for Samantha to park next to him. He pointed to her through his passenger-side window and said, "Stay right there and wait for help."

By the time he got around to the other side, both kids had unbuckled their boosters and were clambering out the back door. Spencer took off running with Michaela right behind.

Do kids ever walk?

As they disappeared through the side gate, leading to the pool and guesthouse in the back, he yelled, "Don't go near the water."

Surprisingly, Sam did as instructed and waited for his assistance. When he opened the door, she dipped her head and looked at him over her wire-rimmed shades.

Sea glass.

Her eyes were the most amazing shade of pale green he'd ever seen... like a beautiful piece of sea glass. He swallowed hard and steadied his breathing, trying not to lose himself in their depth. They flipped from him to the house, widened substantially, which only made them more beautiful, then returned to him.

"Holy Jesus," she said. "This is your house?"

He reached for her hand to help her from the truck, but realized she still had a firm grip on the steering wheel. His blustering and bullying hadn't intimidated her in the slightest, but the monstrous house behind him seemed to have her frozen to the seat.

"No, this isn't my house. This is the Holden estate. I live in the guesthouse in the back."

After a lingering look at the house and a peek toward the backyard, she turned in the seat and allowed him to lift her out by the waist without any argument. Her jaw locked and teeth ground as he set her onto her feet. Her bad foot popped off the concrete driveway and she grabbed the door for support.

"Don't move." He grabbed her straw bag, which appeared to double as a purse and beach bag, and looped it around her neck.

As he picked her up and kicked the door shut, she said, "You don't have to carry me. I can walk."

He suspected the put-me-down rhetoric was pride talking, so he tested the theory by pretending to set her down.

Self-preservation had her grabbing his neck and holding on tight… at least until she realized what she'd done. A surprised gasp caught in her throat and she instantly relaxed her grip, then braced herself for the weight. And the pain.

Damn. Stubbornness was a character trait he knew intimately, but she even had him beat. How bad would she have to hurt before she asked for help?

"I'll keep going," he said as he rounded the front of her truck. "We don't have all day." He chuckled and added, "Well, we do. But I'm not spending it waiting for you to bunny-hop all the way to the back."

Her heavy sigh of relief at not having to walk tugged at his heart.

Her fiercely independent strength touched something inside and made him want to swoop in and protect her. To take care of her so she didn't have to be strong all the time.

"It only took me twenty minutes to get to the truck," she said. "It was a long walk… errr… hop."

"Oh yeah, it's at least fifty yards from the edge of the pavilion to that amazing space I got right at the front of the lot."

"Patience isn't your strong suit, is it?"

Her teasing tone relaxed his guard and without thinking, he laughed and drew her in close for a hug.

A flash of heat ripped through him as her breast pressed against his chest, and when her eyes fixed on his mouth and she bit down on her lip, he nearly stumbled and fell. He drew in a deep, calming breath, but the scent of her shampoo and sunscreen dug deep into his lungs, which only served to send the pulsating energy rippling through him straight to his dick.

Caught in the same current dragging him under, her breathing grew choppy and her arms tightened around his neck as her lips parted, ready and waiting to be kissed. His lips tingled, begging for a touch and a taste of her mouth, while the rest of his body demanded more.

A squeal from the backyard ripped through the magnetic energy pulling them together and broke the spell. He realized he'd stopped in his tracks on the sidewalk and was staring at her like a lovesick teenager—an awkward love-struck teenager who didn't know what the next move should be. The very adult male in him had no hesitations about how to proceed, and based on her reaction, she was right there with him.

Shit, this so wasn't the way to start off an afternoon of maintaining a professional distance and was nothing like hanging out with the guys. He'd never carried Wade around, and he sure as shit never wanted him so badly he could taste it.

Guilt over Lizbeth kick-started his ass and propelled him toward the backyard gate.

Searching for a plausible explanation for his hot-to-cold reaction, he muttered, "The natives are getting restless."

As the gate swung shut behind him, the sound of the lock dropping into place rang out like a shot. So this was what it felt like to be locked in a pen with an exotic animal. Nerve-racking. Exhilarating. Terrifying.

Two weeks… Surely he possessed enough self-control to keep his hands and mouth off her for two weeks.

Chapter Seven

Sam had never seen such a magnificent house, and while fascinated with the site layout, construction, and landscaping, she was intimidated by the enormity. "Who lives here?"

"Cynthia and Max Holden own the property," Kevin said, easing her onto one of the poolside chaise loungers. "Max is currently indisposed, so Cynthia needs help keeping up with everything. Since I split my time between Myrtle Beach and Riverside, I don't need anything bigger than the guesthouse. When their daughter, Callie, moved out, I moved in. The arrangement works well—"

Spencer and Michy burst through the open front door with towels in hand. "Can we go swimming now, Uncle Kevin?"

Kevin turned to Sam. "Can Michaela swim?"

"Yep." She gave Michy her stern-mother face, which Michy returned with an I'm-too-freaking-adorable-to-ever-get-into-trouble grin. "No splashing."

Michy's grin slipped to a pout. "You aren't coming in with us? You got on your bathing suit."

Kevin's head swiveled her way and his eyes lowered, as if trying to confirm visually.

She had no idea what he'd been thinking while carrying her to the backyard, but when he stopped and his hot, hungry eyes devoured her mouth, she nearly orgasmed on the spot. The sexual energy rolling off him had been a powerful shock, paralyzing her lungs. Trapped in his gaze, she couldn't do anything but hold her breath and prepare for his onslaught.

Unfortunately, she'd been spared.

She didn't know if he held back because of the kids, or because he wanted to be a gentleman and not move too fast. Whatever the reason, she hoped they passed that particular roadblock soon, because the real Kevin, in person and on fire, was a million times better than any fantasy.

Knowing he was attracted was the encouragement she needed to move forward with her plan to lure and seduce.

Michy hopped from foot to foot, waiting for Sam's answer.

"I might get in a little later, sweetie." *Right now, I'm going to sit here and work on my diabolical plan.*

The words had barely left her mouth when Michy tossed the towel at her and chirped, "Okay," then turned and ran full-throttle into the pool. Spencer dropped his glasses on top of his towel and ran after her.

"She's devastated I'm not swimming."

Kevin's laugh was deep and throaty. "Yeah, she's real torn up." He picked up Spencer's towel and glasses and set them on the chair before turning toward the house. "I'm gonna grab a beer. Would you like soda, beer,"—he grinned broadly—"whiskey to kill the pain?"

"Wow, you're really going to be my cabana boy." She wasn't sure, but she might've accidentally sighed out loud. "I'm not much of a whiskey girl. The beer sounds great, but I better stick with water. Do you have any ibuprofen?"

"Yes, ma'am." He crossed his arm over his stomach and bowed gallantly. "Coming right up."

Several minutes later, he returned with a bottle of pain reliever and a soft-sided cooler. He unzipped the top, set a Budweiser on the ground at his feet, and grabbed a bottle of water. Holding it out to her, he said, "Sure you don't want something stronger?"

A Miller Lite top peeking out of the ice had her biting her lip, reconsidering. The water would be the smart choice, but if she drank a beer, she'd have another excuse not to drive, at least for a while. Better still, it might give her the courage she needed to make her move.

"Okay, you've convinced me," she said, pointing to the blue and gold cap. "I'll take the Lite, instead."

"Man," Kevin said as he swiped the back of his hand over his brow. "That was a tough sale." He popped the top loose and handed her the bottle. "I have plenty more in the house, so drink all you like."

She grinned and washed the ibuprofen down with the beer. "This'll do me. I'm a cheap drunk on a good day. Combined with the drugs, if I have more than this, Michaela and I will have to crash on your couch."

He chewed the inside corner of his mouth as his gaze crawled from her legs to her neck. After a quick shake of his head and a long, *long* pull on his beer, he swung his legs up on his chaise. He stretched one out in front and bent the one closest to her to use as a prop for his forearm.

"I've been wondering about something."

"My amazing athletic ability?"

His grin was quick and fleeting before he sobered and shook his head. "Tell me about your boots."

What? My boobs?

What the hell was she supposed to say about her boobs?

While she sputtered, looking for an appropriate response, he said, "You've obviously had them for a while and didn't get them strictly for this job."

Oh my God. She burst into laughter. And here she thought he'd be Mr. Smooth-moves. "That's the most original, and ludicrous, come-on

I've ever heard." She slipped her hands under her larger-than-average boobs and gave the girls a proud little lift. "Nope, I didn't get them just for this job. I've had them since I was about eleven, maybe twelve. I don't remember exactly how old."

Kevin's mouth dropped open and his eyebrows rose in surprised interest as his eyes followed the lift and bounce. When the girls settled back into place, he shifted his gaze to hers with the funniest what-the-fuck expression she'd ever seen. He blinked a few times before his face lit up and he threw his head back, laughter pouring out of him. After several moments of unsuccessfully trying to contain his amusement, he took a few deep breaths and wiped his hand over his eyes.

"I think you misunderstood."

He took another deep breath, followed by a long draw on his bottle. After a slow exhale, he seemed satisfied he had himself under control, so he tried again.

"Boots. B-O-O-T-S. Tell me about your boots."

Sam froze with her beer lodged against her lips. "My boots?" Her high-pitched squeak echoed around the bottle as flames licked at her neck and spread over her face.

Shit, he hadn't been coming on to her at all. He was talking about her *work* boots. It was her gutterbrain that turned an innocent question into sexual play. She squeezed her eyes shut and drained her beer.

"I don't know what to say about my boots any more than I did my boobs." She laughed nervously. "Other than to confirm, yes, I've had them for a while… although not quite as long as my boobs. And no, I didn't get them just for this job."

Kevin reached into the cooler, drug another Lite out of the ice, and popped the top. "Here, have another. This is getting good."

She dropped her head in shame and reached for the bottle. "One more, but that's it since I didn't get to finish my lunch. I'll eventually need to drive home, and you may decide sooner is better than later."

He grinned and winked. "Somehow, I doubt that."

Men smiled and winked all the time, but when Mazze did it, an avalanche of excitement rolled in her belly. After her massive misstep, however, she needed to take a breather and regroup before making another advance.

She sipped her fresh beer and nodded to the kids. "I still feel bad you and Spencer left the beach on my account."

Spencer ran the length of diving board and jumped into the water next to Michaela, sending a tidal wave over her head.

"Does he look like he's having a bad time?"

To Spencer, he said, "Hey, what's the rule about running?"

"Don't do it," Spencer said before directing another splash at Michaela. Not to be outdone, she turned her back on him and kicked her feet, soaking him in a barrage of water.

"I'm sorry you're hurt, but this is much better than the beach." His brow drew into a sharp V and his eyes narrowed as he looked at her angry ankle. "You're new in town, right?"

"Yep. Been here about two months."

His gaze slipped to her face. "Do you have family here who can help you over the next few days?"

"Sure." She grinned and nodded to Michaela. "She's a spectacular nurse."

He sighed and a dull expression settled over him. "Not exactly what I had in mind. What about friends?"

"My best friend, Cheri, from high school, lives here." Not that Cheri would be any help this weekend. But when she got back...

"Will she be able to help you get around the next few days?"

She rolled her eyes and readjusted the neck strap on her bathing suit. "I'm not an invalid. It's just a sprain."

"So…" He chewed his lip and slowly nodded. "That's a no. She's not able to help, or you won't ask?"

"Sheesh, you're a pain in the ass." She laughed at his unapologetic shrug. "No, she's not around. She's out of town at a… convention."

She pressed her lips together to keep from grinning at the thought of all the new toys Cheri would bring back from her annual conference. She said they revealed the new items at these events, and Sam was a little too anxious to preview… and sample the new goodies.

"A convention."

Sam giggled. "Yep."

"Why do I get the feeling there's more to this story?"

Heat simmered along her jaw and her heart gave a thwump as she chewed her lip and considered the pros and cons of telling him the truth. This would be a good opportunity to see what he thought about her best friend selling sex toys… and of Sam being her best customer. Would he think she was a kinky freak and lose interest, or would he want to come to her house and play?

After a glance confirmed the kids were out of earshot, she leaned toward him. In a quiet voice, she said, "She has a day job, working for the city. At night, she does in-home parties."

"Like Mary Kay."

Her grin grew. "I don't think Mary Kay ever sold anything like this."

"Interesting."

The longer and more closely he watched her, the more nervous she got.

After several pounding heartbeats, he leaned to the side and met her halfway between their chairs. "Tell me what she sells." His eyes darkened as his gaze locked onto hers. "Exactly."

Whew… even though she sat in the shade, his penetrating stare rocketed her temperature ten degrees higher. This was what happened when you played with matches. What started off as a simple tease burst into a wildfire, trapping her in its midst.

She scratched her temple and brushed a piece of hair away from her eye. "Adult entertainment."

His eyebrow kicked up a notch. "Your friend's a hooker?"

"No!" She huffed and frowned.

It was more of a glare, really, since she suspected he already knew the kind of party to which she referred, but for whatever reason he seemed intent on hearing her say it out loud. She didn't know if he was just being a jerk, or if he was testing her to see how timid and bashful she might be about this kind of thing. Either way, this might be an opportunity to turn the tables and be the lightning strike, rather than the kindling.

She pushed her sunglasses to the top her head, made her eyes heavy and sleepy, and deepened her voice to make it thick and rich. "She sells sex toys at private parties. She's at a conference, learning how to use them."

He grinned at the first part, then jerked his head in surprise and blinked. "I can think of a million ways to learn to use them." His lids dipped and the pulse in his neck jumped as he visually caressed her. "A conference isn't one of them."

"Yeah…" She bit down on her bottom lip and stared at his mouth. A slight breeze ruffled her hair, but did nothing to contain the extreme heat engulfing her. Desperate for relief, she ran the base of the cold bottle across her forehead… down her temple… along the side of her neck and over her shoulder.

Kevin muttered something she didn't understand as he followed her every move. The tension between them grew so thick and taut, it could've been used as a tightrope.

After several uneasy moments, he said, "How about a swim to cool off?" His voice was huskier than before, and she realized he'd moved Spencer's towel over his lap.

She wasn't a cocktease, but after Michael's hatchet job, she'd spent a lot of time questioning her desirability as a woman and her ability to excite a man. Kevin's strong reaction boosted her ego and fragile self-esteem and fueled her naughty little fire.

"Great idea." Especially since it got both of them a little closer to naked.

She sat upright, crossed her arms over her stomach, and took hold of the hem of her T-shirt. She didn't need a degree in stripology to understand the art of a slow reveal, so she made her motions as drawn out and exaggerated as possible. Slowly, she lifted her shirt over her stomach… uncovered her black bikini top… then slipped it over her head. Without being obvious, she glanced at Kevin to check his reaction. A thrill shot through her as his Adam's apple bobbed with a rough swallow and his lips parted, sucking in air.

She protected her ankle by dangling it off the side of the chair, then pushed to her knees and unsnapped her cut-offs. With thumbs hooked inside the waistband, she wiggled side-to-side and eased the shorts over her hips and down her thighs.

Before she got them completely off, Kevin shoved to his feet and stormed off, yammering in a foreign language. She froze, afraid she'd gone too far or miscalculated his interest. But as he crossed the slate patio, she noticed he still had the towel covering the front of his shorts and his breathing was harsh and raspy.

He opened the door on the small utility building that housed the pool mechanicals, tossed a couple noodles to the kids, then grabbed several floats the size of small thrones. He dropped the floats in the water at the pool's edge, then slowly made his way back to her.

When he surrendered the towel to the chair, she couldn't help but glance at his shorts.

Oh, hell yeah. He *was* glad to see her… And she wanted to see more.

"Can you make it to the pool with help, or do you need me to carry you?" His voice was strained, his eyes narrowed, his jaw tight. He seemed to be clamping down on his self-control with an iron fist… which was close to losing its grip.

Had they been alone, she would've kept up the momentum. But, they weren't alone. A fact that was driven home when Spencer bolted from the pool and charged across the deck.

"Yay, you're swimming with us!" He threw his arms around Kevin's waist and tugged, trying to drag his unmovable uncle into the water.

Without saying a word, Kevin picked Spencer up and dropped the squealing child into the pool like he was dumping a load of laundry down a chute. Spencer came up sputtering, then splashed in retaliation as Kevin walked away, laughing.

"After seeing that, I think I'll go it alone."

The corner of his lip kicked up as a sliver of sun broke through the tree branches and reflected off his eyes, making them twinkle. His voice, however, was not light or playful. "I'd handle you with more care."

She gulped as the pulsing attraction arced between them again and propelled her off the chair toward the cool water. At least that was her plan. The second she put the tiniest measure of weight on her foot, numbing pain shot through her ankle and up her leg. Her knee buckled and gravity did the rest, but Kevin snaked his arm around her waist and caught her before she landed.

"Holy sh-sheet, that really hurts."

"It doesn't help to change shit to sheet," he said, his mouth next to her ear. "They're smart kids. They can figure it out."

A shiver raced down her spine as warm breath brushed her ear and neck. She nodded erratically, trying to regain her physical and mental balance. "Baby steps. It takes a long time to change a lifetime of habits." She drew in a fortifying breath and tried going foot-to-ground again.

Kevin stood by, patiently waiting for her to test the ankle, but when it became obvious the pain was too excruciating, he swooped her up and headed toward the stairs.

Startled by the sudden upswing, she squealed and locked her arms around his neck, ensuring if he tried to toss her overboard like Spencer, she'd drag him in with her.

His eyes, no longer red and watery, were sharp and focused, and his nostrils flared as his jaw tightened. She wanted to run her hand along the stubble and ease the tension, but feared the touch would be too intimate… or the proverbial last straw that snapped his control.

Even though she started this game of seduction, she suddenly doubted her ability to ride this bull and wondered if she wouldn't have been smarter sitting this one out.

Chapter Eight

*K*evin's eyes crossed and nearly rolled back in his head as he carried Samantha to the pool. Watching her try to put weight on her injured foot was painful. Having her cradled against him, her arms wrapped around his neck, the fruity flavor of her shampoo making his mouth water and driving him to the edge of insanity with each breath, was excruciating.

The sex toy talk, which sparked a plethora of interesting images and scenarios, had been the proverbial bullet in the chamber. Her boob-swinging, ass-swaying, burlesque-style undressing spun the cylinder. Her nearly naked body plastered against his was like squeezing the trigger in this sexual game of Russian roulette.

The only difference... the consequences of this high-risk game were on a delay, and the survival of his integrity had yet to be determined.

The eventual endgame had already been decided: They would have sex; it would be fantastic. Waiting two weeks to start their physical relationship sounded good in theory. In practice, with an attraction this intense, the only way to make that happen would be to avoid each other, completely.

As he stepped into the cool water and descended the steps, he wondered if Lizbeth was even a factor. For all practical purposes, they were over and done—

You weren't too done last night.

Jesus, how many times would he have to deal with the regret and fallout of the previous night? While sitting in the chair until sunup, watching her sleep and hating himself for being so weak, his conscience beat him bloody. How much more did he need to repent?

He decided to tackle the situation from a different angle. *Would Lizbeth even care?*

If he thought ending their relationship prior to the wedding would be too painful, it was probably a safe bet she'd have a problem with him sleeping with someone else.

Would it matter to Samantha?

He glanced at the woman in his arms… the one studying his jawline and lips with hungry curiosity. He didn't know her well, but he suspected she'd never knowingly get involved with a man already involved with someone else. Even if the other relationship were in its final countdown.

Goddamn him, anyway. Erik was right. He was too nice. Had he ended things with Lizbeth months ago, when the "Dead End" signs first appeared, he wouldn't be in this predicament.

His other option was to throw a few speed bumps at Samantha to slow her down. Several times he'd caught her chewing her lip and tilting her head, as if looking at him from the corner of her eye, checking his reaction. He didn't understand why a strong, beautiful woman would be insecure, but she seemed to be worried about rejection and he didn't want to add to her concern. For that reason, he kept his mouth shut and let her believe he was unattached.

He blew out a breath and wrestled with his conscience. In his heart, he was one hundred percent available—free as a penny lying on the ground, waiting to be picked up. The reality was slightly different, but if he twisted it around…

She tugged the hair at the nape of his neck. "Your ugly facial expression isn't reassuring me I won't get tossed on my ass like Spencer."

"Sorry." He flipped on an it's-all-good smile. "I'm the poster child for ADD. My mind wanders like a curious pup."

He laid her on the float and went back for her beer. Handing it over, he said, "Okay, m'lady. Anything else you need from your cabana boy?"

"That," she said with a grin as she dipped her chin and flipped her gaze to his, "is a loaded question."

He groaned, gritted his teeth, and tried not to focus on the word "load" or think about the one he'd blow if she kept this up. He only had so much willpower, and what little remained was seeping out by buckets.

Her actions seemed innocent enough as she swirled her fingers in the water, then gathered a handful and splashed her neck. But as the rivulets slid across her soft, creamy skin, his breath turned choppy and erratic and his thoughts were far from innocent. One streak ran down the side of her neck and puddled in the hollow above her collarbone, like a pool of water, tempting a man dying of thirst. Another stream slipped over the crest, peaked at the swell of her breast, then streaked down the valley of her deep cleavage.

"Tu non sei un folletta; ma un angelo del sole."

"What language is that?" Michaela asked, doggy paddling over.

He dragged his gaze away from her beautiful mother and smiled. "Italian."

Michaela, reaching shallow enough water to stand, dropped to her feet. Bobbing on tiptoes, she moved her hands back and forth to maintain balance and asked, "What did you say?"

Spencer, also fluent in Italian, would've been able to translate, but he was in the midst of launching a sneak attack on Michaela and hadn't been listening. Kevin glanced at Samantha, who wore an equally curious expression, and scrubbed a hand down his face.

Hell's bells. The temptation to lie was strong, since they'd never know the difference. But that went against his nature, so he took a deep breath and told the truth.

"You're not a pixie; you're a sun angel."

"What?" Sam frowned.

"I wanna be a angel." Michaela paused and her little brow dipped as she thought it over. Turning to her mom, she asked, "What's a pixie?"

Samantha ran her fingers over the top of her ears, as if checking for points, and scrunched up her nose. "Nothing good."

"It's not bad," he said, defensively. Shit, he should've lied. "When you were all up in my grill the other day, so feisty and…" He held his hands out toward her. "Well, you're tiny. With your blond hair and spunky attitude, you reminded me of a pixie. I didn't mean it as a bad thing."

Her eyes narrowed, unconvinced. "Uh-huh, right." She shrugged. "I'm okay with sun angel, though." She brightened and smiled mischievously. "Better yet"—she threw her head back like an obnoxious starlet and shook her ponytail—"a sun goddess."

She bent a knee, dipped her hand in the water, and tossed a handful over her chest. Her nipples tightened as the cold water splashed over them; his cock tightened in response.

Desperate for an escape from the temptation to run his tongue along the water trails and suck the tight buds into his mouth, he let his knees go weak and submersed himself in the cool, refreshing water. He opened his eyes and watched Michaela and Spencer's tiny legs kick back and forth as they doggy paddled and fought over a noodle.

When he ran out of breath and wasn't able to hide any longer, he pushed off the bottom and rose from the water, arms held high, like Poseidon emerging from the sea, and descended upon on them with a mighty roar. One kid squealed—God, he hoped the shrill sound came from Michaela and not his nephew—the other screamed—not much of an improvement over the squeal—and they swam away toward the safety of the deep end.

Go figure.

After a few more attacks on the kids, Kevin left them to entertain themselves and turned his attention to Sam. He pressed his back to the wall and stretched out his arms, hanging on the side of the pool like a barnacle.

Paddling her sun goddess throne over to him, Sam smiled. "Thanks for inviting us over. I still feel bad I ruined your time at the beach, but this is amazing."

"Yeah..." He couldn't agree more, but he let the sentence die, avoiding deeper trouble. "We can do it again tomorrow. Minus the sprain."

Dammit, he needed to get a replacement switch for his mouth's faulty filter. What happened to not getting in deeper?

She laughed and peered down at her leg. "Yeah, I don't *ever* want to do this again."

He watched her peel the label off her bottle and said, "You never told me about your boots." Heavy emphasis on the *t*. "I'm also curious about this lifetime habit of cussing." He laughed as she winced. "I'm guessing you grew up around construction. Am I right?"

Her head fell back against the cushioned headrest and she sighed. A small, sad smile played at her lips, and she nodded. "Yeah. My dad owned a construction company. I spent as much time as I could following him around, learning the business." She laughed. "Both the good and the not-so-great parts… like cussing."

He laughed, remembering all too well the good and the bad habits he'd learned while tagging after his dad. He was seven the first time his mamma washed his mouth out with soap for cursing; by twelve, she'd given up.

"My dad wouldn't let me go with him until I was big enough to climb into the cab of his truck by myself. The climbing in part wasn't the problem. Reaching the handle, then having enough strength to push the button and open the door was something else entirely."

He glanced at the mini-Sam attempting to reach the diving board so she could hang from it while Spencer jumped off. He had no problem picturing Sam as a kid.

"How old were you when you finally got the door open?"

"Almost five." She smiled broadly, obviously still taking pride in pulling off such a big feat for a little girl. "I wasn't allowed to cheat and stand on anything, other than my tippy-toes. I tried every single day, and the day I finally got that da… danged door open was better than any Christmas morning."

She stared into the distance and laughed. "I can still see the shock on Daddy's face when he climbed into the cab with his thermos and lunch bucket and found me sitting on the seat. I was covered in dirt and grease from head to toe, because after I got the door open, I had to crawl onto the floorboard and then up onto the seat."

"Did he take you with him?"

"Oh yeah. A deal was a deal. He went back into the house to tell Mama she had the day free and came back with an extra sandwich and a bottle of juice for my lunch."

The pleasure rippling off her seeped into his chest.

"Do you have siblings?"

The change in her was drastic as the smile fell from her face and her shoulders sagged. "Yeah. Three older brothers."

He waited for her to say more, to give insight into why his question leached the pleasure out of her, but none came. "Were they as anxious to go to work with your dad?"

"Hel-heck no." She shook her head emphatically. "They could've cared less. My oldest brother didn't like to get dirty. My middle brother was too interested in sports. My younger brother was, and still is, a bum."

She took a long pull on the beer. "They didn't give a rat's ass about the business." Along with the increasing tension in her body, her voice shook with a biting edge.

Kevin debated dropping the inquisition, but he wanted to know more about her. Settling on middle ground, he switched back to a topic he hoped made her smile again.

"What was your dad's specialty?"

"Builder, like you. We were out of Columbia. I don't think our paths ever crossed, but I heard the Mazze name a lot. Especially as I got older and started taking on more responsibilities. Daddy handled all the estimating." She gave a half-smirk. "When you outbid us, I definitely heard your name, usually combined with colorful adjectives."

She worked in the same field as him and their paths never before crossed? "What was the name of your company?"

"Seymore Builders."

The inside of his ears twitched, like an animal's hearing a familiar sound. "Chas was your dad?" His arms went slack and he almost fell off the side of the pool as a million mental puzzle pieces got dumped on the floor all at once.

She nodded and gulped. "Yeah."

He scrambled, trying to fit the right piece in the right slot, sorting through the rumors and what he believed to be fact. Chas was a great guy. Everyone had been stunned and felt the loss when he'd dropped dead of a heart attack on his way to work one morning.

"I'm sorry, Samantha. I thought a lot of your dad. He was well respected by everyone."

Her smile returned, only not as sharp and crisp. "Thanks. That's nice to hear. And, please, call me Sam. I despise Samantha."

He grinned. Why was that not a surprise?

"Why didn't you continue the business after his passing? I remember hearing speculation you would." He paused and took in her crumpled expression and hollow eyes. "Everyone believed you more than capable of carrying on in his footsteps."

"Not everyone." She took a long drink of her beer, which had to be warm and nasty, but she didn't seem to care. "My dad messed up."

He cocked his head to the side, sure he misunderstood. "What?"

"He didn't have a proper will in place, so when he died, everything went to my mother. My brothers convinced her I wouldn't be able to run the business, at least not profitably. So, they helped her"—she made quotations marks with her fingers—"liquidate everything, and my oldest brother, who is an accountant, handled the financial end of things. My mom gets a monthly stipend, and after she passes, whatever is left will get divided between us kids"—she huffed and her shoulder twitched—"or at least them."

He pulled his jaw back into place and blinked a couple of times. "They sold the business out from under you, without giving you an opportunity to prove yourself?"

"Yep." She twisted her mouth around and chomped down on her upper lip. "My ex didn't help matters. Michaela was little, and he thought it would be best if I stayed home with her. They all joined forces and… as they say… the rest is history."

Kevin was shocked into silence. He knew Chas's company dissolved after his death, but he hadn't gotten any details. He'd heard rumors, and sadly enough, it seemed some were pretty damned close to the truth. He couldn't believe she'd been dumped on the street.

"I'm struck stupid, Sam. I don't even know what to say. I can't imagine if my sister and mother did something like that to me." Of course, they wouldn't, since his sister was the office manager and both of his parents had complete faith in him.

That had to be what hurt Sam the most. Siblings shitting on you was one thing, but to have her own spouse and mother betray her? Christ, that must have made a deep and long-lasting mark.

Without conscious thought to his actions, or to the consequences, he drew her raft to him and stroked his hand down her leg. He wished he'd known her then so he could've offered comfort and support and helped ease her pain.

Keep his hands to himself for two weeks? Hell, he hadn't made it two hours. But he didn't care. He saw vulnerability in her for the first time, and he wanted her to know he had her back.

Though barely five feet tall, she projected an image of being twice that height and bulletproof. Even while rolling around on the ground in agony, she'd been prepared to kick ass and take names, rock-solid and ready to battle the world if necessary.

Now… she had the appearance of someone who *had* battled the world, tried to kick ass and take names, but was badly beaten. She appeared small, isolated, and exceptionally lonely.

"For what it's worth, I have no doubt you were more than capable of running your old man's business. I'm sure you would've made him proud."

Her shoulders rose with her deep inhale and the corner of her mouth lifted. "Thanks." She played with a puddle of water that gathered on her float. "This probably sounds silly, and it's a completely different situation, but I wish someone had thrown me a life raft when I needed it. That's why I took you home last night… I mean…" Her face flushed. "I took your *file* home last night and spent some time, umm"—her lips twitched as she glanced away—"working up options for you and Wade to look over when we meet on Monday."

Kevin stared, dumbfounded and nearly speechless for the second time in five minutes. "You worked on my project last night?"

"Yeah, it wasn't any big deal. Michy and I did our normal Friday night thing. We ate pizza and drank beer while watching our requisite Friday night movie." She rolled those big eyes to him. "*Beauty and the Beast,* in case you were wondering." She laughed. "I guess I should clarify. She had root beer. I had the real thing. Anyway, after I got her to bed, I didn't have anything else to do, so I sat down to work. I enjoyed it."

All he could do was stare and keep pushing breath in and out. She'd spent her Friday night at home, drinking beer and eating pizza, watching a movie with mini-Sam, working on his project. He'd never seen a Disney movie—at least not that he remembered—but aside from that, she'd had the opportunity to enjoy a perfect Friday night, relaxing and doing nothing. Instead, she worked on his project.

Meanwhile, he spent the night cinched into a suit, feeling out of place in his own home, surrounded by strangers, with a woman who was going to be the death of him.

He turned, lifted himself out of the pool, and bolted for the cooler. He'd been having so much fun with Sam and the kids, other than the beer he drank when they first arrived, he hadn't considered having another. He hadn't even finished the first one. But now, thoughts of Lizbeth sent him running for an ice-cold Bud like his life depended on it.

As he knelt down, a gust of air blew over his wet skin, chilling him to the bone. He paused with the top of the cooler partially unzipped, recognizing this was a defining moment. Did he want to continue down this path, or did he want to take a different road?

He looked over his shoulder at Sam sitting on her float, completely bewildered by his quick escape. He watched the kids wrestling over the other float, laughing and playing and having a great time without a care in the world. He looked at the massive house casting a shadow over the pool and thought of Max Holden and all he'd lost because of bad choices.

Kevin was close, real fucking close, to crossing the line that could jeopardize everything he'd ever worked for and everything he'd ever wanted.

He closed his eyes and took a few deep breaths, swallowing the panic rising in his chest. He re-zipped the cooler and pushed it under his chair, hoping out of sight would be out of mind. He wanted to make different choices in every segment of his life. Choices that would allow him to take better care of himself and find happiness, rather than always putting someone else first.

The concept was so foreign, a large part of him balked at the idea. He felt like a selfish asshole, but he had to talk to Lizbeth. Forget all the reasons he had for not ending things with her, his quality of life demanded otherwise.

She had to see the writing on the wall, and it wasn't right to continue when they were never going to be more than they were now. He wasn't going to risk losing something that might be special just because he didn't want to hurt Lizbeth.

New choices. New roads.

After a quick prayer for strength and the release of guilt, he slipped back into the water next to Sam, who studied him from the corner of her eye, wary and confused. He rested his forearm on the opposite side of the raft and leaned over her. "Thank you."

"It wasn't a big deal. Really."

It was a big deal. He was so grateful she'd shown up in his life, even if their first two meetings had been costly for both of them. But he decided to leave her thinking it was all about Vanguard.

He had no idea what the future held, but he wanted it to look like her.

Her eyes roamed over his face, studying him a little too closely for comfort, but he didn't back off or look away. After a moment, she said, "What just happened?"

While he didn't feel the need to hide, he also didn't see a need for full disclosure. Besides, what would he say? *I'm on the verge of being an alcoholic, although I'm realizing it's more of a situation thing. With you, I'm happy and don't need to drink. But when I think about my girl-friend—oh yeah, have I failed to mention her?—I want to guzzle by the gallons.*

Yeah. Not.

He smiled and shook his head, shrugging off her question, then stepped back, giving her some space. "Nothing."

He ran his hand over her uninjured foot and down the sole. She closed her eyes and moaned with pleasure as he ran his thumb up her arch, then circled it over the pad below her toes.

He'd avoided crossing one line today, but as he rubbed her foot and enjoyed the ecstasy etched on her face, he slid into dangerous territory. The boundaries between right and wrong were blurring. A smart man would remove his hand from her leg, take a step back, and make sure he maintained at least ten feet of distance between them at all times, at least until after he'd talked to Lizbeth.

However, he'd apparently lost all sensibilities, because rather than removing his hand, he leaned in closer and said, "You went above and beyond for me. Now let me do something for you. Let me stay with you and Michy tonight, so I can take care of you."

Chapter Nine

*T*wo hours after The Incident, as Sam had come to think of it, she still hadn't figured out what launched Kevin out of the pool and across the deck like his ass was on fire and the ice in the cooler was his only chance at survival. But since then, he'd been a perfect cabana boy, seeing to her every need while she reclined on the lounger, her leg propped up on a pillow covered in a luxurious, multi-million thread-count pillowcase, an ice pack wrapped around her ankle, with a glass of lemonade… complete with a little umbrella Kevin found in the kitchen cabinet—a leftover from Callie. Or so he claimed.

After announcing his intentions to stay with her for the night, he'd spent several moments convincing her she needed to stay off her ankle so it would heal faster. The best way to do that, of course, would be with his help. She didn't accept help easily, but the heat flaring in his eyes as he said, "So I can take care of you," had done more to convince her than anything else.

Although the subject of sex hadn't come up, an excited rush skittered across her shoulders as she thought about what the night might bring. She hoped like hell his idea of caretaking amounted to more than making tomato soup and grilled cheese sandwiches for dinner.

The side gate opened and a tall, dark-haired woman stepped into the backyard. Spencer jumped out of the pool and rushed her. "Mamma, I don't want to go. I want to stay here with Uncle Kevin and

Michaela and Ms. Sam. Can I, please?"

His mother's gaze slid across the patio to Michaela, who clamored out of the pool to serve as Spencer's backup, then to Sam. She wore an odd expression as she cut her eyes to Kevin, then turned back to Spencer.

"Sorry, buddy. Uncle Kevin left a message saying you guys were here instead of the beach. I tried calling back, but I didn't get an answer, so I decided to come on over and find you. Since I'm here, you need to come with me."

"Sorry," Kevin said. "I've had my phone on vibrate."

His sister arched her brows and opened her mouth, but Kevin gave a sharp shake of his head to cut her off as Spencer leapt in with more begging.

"Please, Mamma. Why can't I stay?"

Kevin tossed him up over his shoulder in a fireman's carry. "Your mamma said it's time to go." He spun around so he faced Marianne and mouthed, "Can he come back tomorrow?"

"Sure." She shrugged. "Other than mass, I don't have any plans."

Kevin gave Spencer a hug and set him on his feet. "Your mamma says you can come back tomorrow, but only if you behave tonight. Deal?"

Spencer stuck out his tiny fist and bumped Kevin's. "Deal. Is Michaela gonna be here tomorrow too?"

"Uh…" Kevin spun around to Sam. "Yes?"

Only a fool would pass up the opportunity to do this again. "Sure."

"Yay." Michy and Spencer celebrated the victory while a strange vibe passed between Kevin and his sister.

Sam realized she and Michaela hadn't been introduced, so maybe his sister was trying to figure out who the strays in Kevin's yard were, without coming right out and asking.

"I'm Sam, by the way. Michaela and Spencer go to afterschool together." She pushed to a sitting position and began to stand, then glanced down and stopped. "I've wanted to talk to you about arranging some playdates with the kids, but I'm usually too late to catch you."

Marianne winced as she approached. "Ow, that looks painful." Extending her hand, she said, "I'm Marianne Mazze. Spencer talks about Michaela all the time. It'd be great to get them together." Marianne turned to Kevin and grinned. "Maybe we could leave both kids with Kevin sometime and grab lunch or something."

Sam felt her eyes light up. "That sounds wonderful."

Kevin rocked back on his heels and smiled at Marianne. "Maybe *you* could keep both while Sam and I grab dinner."

Marianne's mouth went slack, but she quickly recovered. "Uh, sure. I could do that." She grabbed Spencer's towel and glasses from the chair. "Okay, buddy. Let's go. Where's your shoes?"

After gathering his shoes and change of clothes from the house, Spencer told Sam good-bye, then ran to the gate where his mom and Kevin waited.

"Sam, it was nice to meet you." As she freed the latch on the gate, Marianne frowned and asked Kevin, "Can you help me with something real quick?"

He exhaled sharply and nodded. "Of course."

He ruffled Michy's hair, who'd run to the gate, looking like her best friend was leaving forever. "Don't look so sad, *piccolina*. He'll be back tomorrow." He nodded to Sam. "I'll be right back and we can figure out what's for dinner."

"More than tomato soup and grilled cheese?" Sam asked hopefully.

Kevin crinkled his nose and chuckled. "Yeah. I'd planned on more than that."

Sam's smile grew as she mentally rubbed her hands together. *Me, too.*

Kevin knew this conversation was inevitable, but he'd hoped to avoid it until Monday. Marianne, however, had less patience than him, and his hope had only been a pipe dream.

While she helped Spencer into the car, cranked the engine so the air conditioner would keep him cool, then shut the door to block his little ears from the conversation, Kevin stood by like a child, waiting to be lectured.

"You want to fill me in on what's going on with your life, because I've obviously missed a few important changes."

Kevin shook his head and studied the expansion joint in the concrete driveway. "You haven't missed anything, sis. This isn't exactly what it looks like."

"What *exactly* is it?"

"Sam's a building inspector… the same one who shut us down yesterday."

Marianne crossed her arms over her chest and nodded. "I see."

Okay, that wasn't the reaction he expected. How could she see anything when he still fumbled around in the dark? "You see… what?"

"You're making nice and letting her kid swim in your pool so she'll give us the CO."

"What?" He drew back and did Erik's squint-for-clearer-focus thing again. Which was absolutely ridiculous, because this particular move hadn't proved any more effective than counting backward from ten. "No."

Marianne rolled her eyes and pressed one hand to the hood of his truck while propping the other on her hip.

"Michaela and Spencer go to afterschool—"

"I got that part."

He ran his tongue over the front of his teeth and glared. "You ready to let me finish?"

"Go ahead," she said while spiraling her hand, motioning for him to continue.

"The kids had a plan to meet up at the Boardwalk today. Amazingly enough, it worked out. But Sam fell and sprained her ankle, so I brought them back here so the kids could still play."

"And... based on the dinner comment, Kevin has plans to play as well."

As his jaw creaked from the extreme pressure, she threw her palm out defensively. "Hey, I don't care. I've never understood the Lizbeth thing anyway. I always figured it came down to great sex because that's the only thing you guys could possibly have in common. I'm just curious what's going on and wondering if Lizbeth knows she's been replaced."

"She doesn't know—She hasn't been—I just..." His shoulders slumped.

Just what? There wasn't any denying his attraction to Sam. Hell, he'd been attracted to her yesterday when she shut his shit down. Today, she definitely wasn't shutting him down in any way, and the already intense attraction had only grown.

Her two-piece bathing suit that revealed the perfect amount of cleavage while providing enough coverage to make his imagination work overtime drove his testosterone level through the roof and inspired all kind of XXX thoughts. The bedroom eyes she'd tossed his way, as well as the heat continually building between them, let him know she was ready and willing. All he had to do was take.

But the more time he spent with her, the more he learned about her, the more he watched her with Michaela and Spencer...

The more he wanted more.

Sex, at this point, was a given. He was still hoping for the strength to make it until after he'd ended things with Lizbeth. But he also recognized sex alone wouldn't be enough. He didn't want just her body; he wanted the woman.

He'd decided no more quick lays or one-nighters. He wanted to do things differently. And he wanted to start that new plan with Sam.

Marianne drummed her fingers on the hood of the car and tapped her toe once, waiting for him to finish explaining himself.

He didn't know how to make Marianne understand any of that, so he went with what he knew. "I've wanted to break things off with Lizbeth for a while, but it didn't feel right because of the wedding. Things would be awkward for the entire wedding party, and it seemed unfair to Wade and Miranda. Not to mention being cruel to Lizbeth."

"Yeah," Marianne said with a twitch of her nose. "Knowing Lizbeth and her dramatics, she'd make such a big deal out of it, she'd completely ruin the day for Miranda—"

"Exactly!" Kevin exhaled with relief at Marianne's understanding. "Erik says I've waited this long, another two weeks won't kill me, but..." He glanced to the backyard and envisioned the woman in a black two-piece with the sea-green eyes, glistening with sunscreen.

"The way you looked at her, and listening to you talk just now, I can see there's something special about her. It seems awful risky to me, and you don't want to screw up something that might be a good thing."

He didn't want to think like that. He hadn't done anything wrong, at least not yet. At this point, he could even share the details of his day with Lizbeth—minus the few stumbles and micro meltdowns.

"Hey." He spun around to Marianne. "Do you know who her dad

is?"

Marianne, figuring this wasn't a serious question, but a quick diversionary tactic, gave him the don't-be-stupid expression she'd mastered as a toddler. "I didn't know her until five minutes ago."

He smiled arrogantly. "Chas Seymore."

Her eyebrows shot up as her mouth dropped open. "No shit." She glanced at the backyard gate. "Wow, I've wondered what happened to her. I thought she'd take over after he died, but then... she disappeared. What's she doing here?" She pulled an ugly face. "Why's she working as an inspector?"

A wave of sadness crested in his chest as he remembered the isolation and defeat surrounding the normally rock-solid woman in his backyard. "Long story, but her family sold the business out from under her. I think she'd like to get back into building. We've been looking for a floating foreman who can fill in on jobs while the regular foreman is out, like while Wade is out on his honeymoon. She'd be perfect for the job."

"Yeah, she would. Except after shit hits the fan with you guys, I'll be left dealing with a disgruntled, hysterical female."

Shit won't hit the fan was his first thought, but he said, "Nope. She's just like you. Exacting painful revenge is more her style. No hysterical female dramatics, I promise."

"In that case," she said, giving him a hug, "she and I will get along just fine." She stepped back and opened her door. "You want me to do some checking around, just to make sure we're not missing something before we make the offer?"

Kevin grinned. He'd had the idea of hiring Sam as soon as he learned who she was. He hadn't intended to broach the subject with Marianne so soon and had actually been using it as a smokescreen to get her off the subject of his increasingly fucked-up personal life. But

Marianne was as passionate about their company as him, and if he had an idea she thought worthwhile, she'd explore it to the fullest.

He couldn't imagine what it would be like to have her knock the foundation out from under him and leave him standing in the cold. His gaze shifted to the gate. Rather than the sexual urges he was growing accustomed to battling, his protective Mr. Fix-it showed up at the door.

Sam's family had treated her horribly, but their loss would be his gain. He had no doubt she would make a great addition to Mazze Builders.

He just prayed she also made an awesome addition to his personal life.

Chapter Ten

Sam couldn't remember the last time she had such an enjoyable day. Despite the steady bass beating in her ankle, she'd laughed and played like she didn't have a care in the world. Based on the smile in Kevin's eyes as he helped her and Michy into his truck, and his comments about looking forward to doing it again the next day, she supposed he had a good time, too. Now here they were, riding home in his truck, with Kevin's overnight bag sitting next to Michy and a flock of butterflies riding shotgun in Sam's gut.

"Turn at the next right," she said, pointing to the green street sign coming into view. "We're the second house on the left."

Their house was small, with a marginally larger yard, in an average neighborhood far away from the grandeur and opulence of Kevin's. She couldn't complain. She felt fortunate to have found the little two-bedroom bungalow so soon after moving, but the differences between Kevin's lifestyle and hers were striking.

He turned onto the busted concrete driveway, killed the engine, and peered over his shoulder at Michy. Exhausted from a big day of playing, she'd fallen asleep as soon as they hit the road. Her head had flopped so far forward it appeared to be in danger of rolling off her shoulders, and a line of drool rolled off her bottom lip. The corner of Kevin's mouth lifted in a sweet smile and his eyes turned melted-chocolate soft as he swiped his hand across her chin, mopping up the mess.

Sam's heart stopped, then chugged to life at the tender gesture shown by a man they barely knew and so much sweeter than anything Michael ever did. Until this moment, she never realized how strained life with him had been and how much she and Michy missed.

"Give me your keys and I'll unlock the house," he said, stretching out his hand. "I'll come back and carry her to bed."

"Good luck," Sam said with a snort as she dug her keys from her bag. "She usually wakes up as soon as the vehicle stops." She cocked her head and studied Michy… who hadn't so much as fluttered an eyelash.

He glanced at Sleeping Beauty and smiled. "I love a challenge… I'm not so sure this'll be one, though."

While he unlocked the house and turned on lights, Sam crawled out of the truck… slowly and carefully, making sure to keep her foot elevated.

"You want me to get her or help you first?"

Holding the side of the truck, she hopped out of the way and made room for him to get Michaela out of the back. "You get her and I'll get me."

With a huff and a half-eye roll, he said, "You're more stubborn than I am, and that's saying something."

"What?" she said, hopping around to the front of the truck, proving her point. "I got this. No problem."

"What're you going to do when you don't have the truck to hold on to?"

"Hold the bushes."

He stepped back and peeked around the door at the scrawny, barely-there azaleas. "This'll be good." He took in the neighboring houses. "I bet I could sell tickets."

He eased Michaela out of her seat, wrapped one hand around the back of her head to hold her against his shoulder, and cradled her close to his chest. His careful attentiveness tugged at Sam's heart and made her glad Michy was asleep so this man's magnetic charm didn't weave the same magic around her daughter that it cast over her.

As soon as he disappeared into the house, Sam doubled her efforts to get around the front of the truck and up the sidewalk before he returned. The scraggly azaleas were short—even by her measure—so they weren't as useful as she planned. She grabbed twigs and tendrils where she could, but it came down to hoping for the best and allowing momentum to propel her along.

Three hops away from the handrail, Kevin reappeared in the doorway. "I assume her room is the one with the pink princess shit everywhere."

With broken concentration, she hobbled and bobbled and nearly went over. She grabbed for the handrail as Kevin grabbed her, and together they managed to keep her upright. Once on steady footing, she grimaced and nodded. "Isn't it awful? How did I end up with such a girly girl?"

With a cramping spasm shooting up her good calf, into her thigh, and toward her butt, she studied the steps and sighed. "Okay, I give. Will you help me?"

"Sure, but it'll cost you." His deep and menacing tone caused her to snap her gaze to his. A smile played on his lips, but his eyes were dark and serious, his body tense.

She worked her tongue around the roof of her mouth, manufacturing moisture so she could answer. "How much?"

"I'm pretty cheap, so not much," he said, lifting her in his arms. He shut the door behind them, flipped the lock, and veered right into the living room. "In here?"

She considered telling him to skip the couch and take her directly to bed, but she'd been forward enough with her previous flirtatious advances. He knew she was interested. Hell, he knew she was a sure thing. They'd already established he'd be staying the night under the guise of helping with her foot—at least she hoped it was just a cover story—so she wanted to back off and let him run the show from here on out. If he wanted to start off on the couch watching football, she was down with that.

God, please let him be a Clemson fan and not a South Carolina Gamecock. She wouldn't be able to bear hearing "Let's go Cocks" streaming from his mouth.

Between dinner and the ride home, her foot had been down for a while, so the swelling and throbbing had gotten worse.

Catching her wince, he said, "You get settled here. I'll get you an ice pack and pillow to prop up your leg. Where can I find one?"

She rested her head against the arm of the sofa and stretched out, hating herself for being a wimp. But the ibuprofen quit working hours ago and she really hurt. She smiled at the man hovering over her with concern marring his handsome face. She wasn't accustomed to letting anyone take care of her, but she liked knowing someone cared.

"There's a bag of frozen peas in the freezer that'll work well. I keep spare pillows and blankets in the bottom drawer of my dresser. You can grab one of those."

"I'm sure you're not used to letting anyone take care of you. Thanks for allowing me to do this." He pressed a kiss to her forehead and walked away.

She ran her fingers over her forehead like she could capture the kiss and hold it in place. His lips had been as soft as she suspected, and she couldn't wait for a real kiss. Just as she'd imagined last night—

Fuck!

As his footsteps disappeared into her bedroom, panic seized her. She'd gotten a new dresser when she moved into this house and this one only had one bottom drawer. She also had a hall closet now, so she moved the blankets and pillows to the closet and used the bottom dresser drawer for her *toys*.

"Kevin," she yelled, scrambling off the couch and landing on her ass with a thud. "Kevin, stop." She used the coffee table to get to her foot and hopped around the end table. She grabbed the back of the rocking chair, which was not the least bit helpful, then bunny-hopped down the hallway. She wanted to yell again, but was afraid of waking Michy. However, if she didn't yell, Kevin would—

She rounded the bedroom door as the bottom drawer slid open for the full reveal.

The rhetorical question she asked on the boardwalk had been answered. The day *could* get more embarrassing; her mortification was complete.

The wheels of time ground to a screeching halt… stood still for several heartbeats… then, one cog at a time, began to turn in slow motion. His eyes widened in surprise at not finding a pillow and blanket as expected, but a mass profusion of eroticism that would make a seasoned hooker blush. He blinked once, then twice as his nostrils flared and his chest rose and fell with sharp, heavy breaths. His head swiveled toward her, and he trained nearly black eyes on her face.

Her cheeks flamed, and she wanted to turn and flee from the room as fast as her hop-along gait would allow, but she was locked in place, held captive by his intense stare. Besides, even if she could escape, where would she go? Running back to the couch wouldn't undo any of this or magically make him forget what he saw.

She shifted her weight, trying to ease the pressure on her heel, but he must've thought she was preparing to bolt because he said, "Don't move."

His command, delivered in a rough, raspy voice, made her good leg go weak, and she grabbed hold of the waist-high dresser for balance.

"These are things your friend sells?"

She swallowed again and went for a joke, hoping to ease a little of the tension. "I'm a quality control tester. If I give a good rating, she sells it. If not…" She shrugged and glanced at the leather slapper in his hand.

"Can I assume you only keep the good stuff, or…," he picked up the Long Dong and flipped his eyes to her, "…does the bad stuff settle to the bottom while your favorites stay on top?"

She flicked her attention to the paddle and chewed her bottom lip. "Something like that."

He replaced the vibrator and traced a pattern in the wood-grain paddle, as she'd done the night before. She tried to settle her choppy breathing by drawing in deep, uneven breaths, but it was a losing battle.

"What's your favorite?"

She glanced at the Double Dong and shook her head. *Oh, hell no.* It was bad enough he learned she had a whole drawer full of this stuff; no way would she share her deepest secrets. She didn't need to vocalize anything, however. Her eyes had given her away.

He picked up the double dildo and his eyebrows arched dramatically. His throat pumped a few times before he cleared it and said, "Can you take this whole thing, sugar?"

She pressed her lips together and willed her body not to betray her further.

"I'm taking your silence as a yes. Interesting…"

She pressed her palms against the dresser, preparing to push into an upright position. In a quick, fluid motion, Kevin had the paddle in his hand, the bedroom door shut, and stood next to her, blocking her path.

"Your eyes went to this paddle a half dozen times." He ran his hand along the smooth, beveled edge. "I don't know anything about Cheri's toys, but I do know wood. This nice, cherry paddle wasn't mass-produced. Where'd you get it?"

"A show in Charlotte."

His eyes narrowed and his mouth worked while he chewed the inside of his cheek. He stepped closer and pressed his body against her side. "You enjoy being spanked?"

She turned her head to hide her face and shrugged. "I don't know."

"Look at me."

His voice was sharp and commanding, and he said nothing else while waiting for her to follow his directive. She looked back to him, but his dark eyes seemed to bore straight into her soul and she couldn't maintain eye contact.

"What do you mean you don't know?"

Jesus, would the horror never end? He'd found her stash, identified her favorite toy, and figured out the paddle didn't come from Cheri's, which meant she'd gone out of her way to buy that specific implement—which would make him believe she enjoyed being spanked. But the truth was she didn't know. She'd never been spanked by anyone but herself.

Could one get any more pathetic?

Refusing to bare her soul any further, she pushed off the dresser and away from him.

Before she could open the door, his arm shot out and wrapped around the front of her waist, locking her in place to prevent an escape while supporting her weight so she didn't put pressure on her foot. "Did your husband use these toys on you?'

Her harsh laugh was answer enough.

He tilted his head and studied her closely. "Has anyone ever spanked you?"

When she didn't answer, he gave her a quick, sharp swat with the paddle. It didn't hurt, but shocked her, making her gasp and glare simultaneously. His tone was low and authoritative, a different person than the easy-going, playful man she spent the afternoon with.

"Answer me or you'll get another."

Well now, wasn't this an interesting conundrum? If she didn't answer, he'd spank her, which was exactly what she wanted. A win-win-win.

The corner of his mouth notched up. "That's what I thought."

"Oh, you're a mind reader now?" Reflexes and a sense of preservation had her fighting, even though she didn't really want to go anywhere. Her muscles contracted as her internal struggle persisted.

His chin dipped and he looked through the fringe of his lashes with soft, understanding eyes. "I have a friend who owns a kink club. I did some work for him and spent a fair amount of time at the club with him and his wife." He lifted a shoulder casually. "I've picked up a few things over the years."

He maneuvered his body behind hers, pressed his hands to the sides of her hips, and positioned her at the end of the dresser. Leaning over her back, he whispered in her ear, "Palms on the dresser, ass up and out. Let's find out how much you enjoy this."

Excitement and cold panic raced down her spine as excessive heat warnings went out to the rest of her body. Despite her embarrassment, fear, and trepidation, she did as he said. She didn't know when she might have another chance like this, and she didn't want to miss the opportunity.

Her slick palms slid on the dresser, so she drove them into the wood surface, anchoring herself in place. Bent over like this with her butt stuck out, the only thing missing was a plaid skirt and a half-unbuttoned white top and she'd be the perfect misbehaving schoolgirl. Instead, she wore cut-off shorts and a pink T-shirt. Standing barefoot, with her bad foot tucked up and under, she probably looked like a friggin' flamingo.

Thoughts of feathered friends, pink or otherwise, fled when he stroked a hand down her back, over her butt, and down her thigh. Terror and euphoria simultaneously ripped through her system, creating a jumbled mass of nerves that had her locked arms shaking so badly she feared they might not continue to support her weight.

He brushed a piece of hair from her face and kissed her temple as he ran the paddle around her butt in a circle. "We're just playing, Sam. Relax."

She nodded, closed her eyes, and drew in a deep breath, using his unique scent to ground her. When the first blow landed, she jumped, then dropped her head back with a sigh. She might've whispered, "More," but she wasn't sure if she'd thought it or if her lips actually parted, allowing the word to slip out. Heat built with each blow as the paddle landed a second, third, and forth time. She sucked in through her teeth and bit her bottom lip to keep from crying out as the sting spread into a slow burn over her entire backside.

Another crack had her head falling forward and her body quaking so heavily she'd probably register on the Richter scale. And that was before he unsnapped and unzipped her shorts, then slid his hand along her stomach and into her bathing suit bottoms.

"Oh God. That feels so good" Her voice was barely above a whisper as she struggled to catch her breath and keep herself vertical. "I can't keep standing."

His hand continued its southern descent until his fingers skimmed over her clit and slid through the slick folds of her sex. "You can and you will."

He pushed two fingers inside, pressed the heel of his hand against her pubic bone, and anchored the weight of her body against his forearm. "Shit, you're so wet. I'd say we answered the question about whether or not you like to be spanked."

Her sex clenched around his fingers as another stinging swat from the paddle combined with the pressure of his fingers inside and his palm against her clit, sending her to the edge of an exquisite release. "More. One more, please."

"Look at me."

When she did, he captured her mouth with his and nearly kissed the life out of her. His tongue drove into her mouth, and he obliged with not one, not two, but three quick strikes that sent her flying. He fed her breath when she gasped for air and swallowed her screams as the orgasm ripped through her.

He dropped the paddle and, true to his word, held her tightly with both arms until the waves subsided, not only making sure she didn't fall, but fully supporting her weight so she didn't have to do anything but feel good. When she began to settle, he slowly withdrew his fingers, sending out a few aftershocks and keeping her in a highly sensitized state.

When she was no longer gasping for air and could speak coherently, she said, "That was amazing." She cut her eyes to the side and gave a wicked little grin. "More."

Chapter Eleven

*K*evin flipped the blue and gray satin comforter back and carefully laid Sam on the bed. Standing upright, he pushed his hand through his hair and drew in a few ragged breaths, trying to gather his wits. The odds had been stacked against him from the beginning, but when he opened that fucking drawer, it was like having a vault blown wide open, nothing standing between him and all the riches in the world. All the checks and balances and logical thinking that were instilled in him over his lifetime were eviscerated, and there was nothing and no one to stop him from taking what he wanted.

Sam was a beautiful woman he was drawn to on so many levels. She was willing to go as far as he wanted, and she had a drawer full of toys to make the ride all the more thrilling.

His only hesitation came when her eyes fixated on the paddle. His blood ran lava hot, then ice cold… at least until he figured out her rationality behind the stash and determined whether she simply enjoyed variety and play with her sex, or if the implements were necessary to fulfill a dark, deep-seated compulsion.

He'd spent enough time with Lucas at the club, experimenting and playing with subs, to acknowledge bondage and discipline were activities he found highly erotic—especially the discipline.

Then he'd gotten involved with Lizbeth and all that changed. She didn't want to "play" for fun. She needed her sex rough, almost combative. He'd been okay with the hard stuff in the beginning, but her constant need to push harder stopped being erotic and turned into a battle of wills. Who could push the hardest? Who would break first?

He'd played with the paddle and strap, watching Sam's reaction, trying to figure out where she fell on the want versus need spectrum. He'd taken classes at the club to learn the proper techniques and worked with subs, learning to read their responses to best traverse their emotional landscape. The look on Sam's face reminded him of a few of those subs. She wasn't ashamed of her predilection, but feared being rejected because of it.

He'd surmised this was a desire to experiment, rather than a need, something she confirmed by admitting she'd never actually been spanked.

And hadn't that revelation sent his junkyard dog to the end of his chain, snarling and growling until the links snapped and he was on the loose.

The more he stroked her ass with the paddle, the raspier her breath became and the harder her heart pumped. Her carotid artery beat so hard against the side of her neck, the damned thing looked like it was trying to escape.

What he found most interesting, though, was his physical response to her excitement. He'd enjoyed working with subs at the club, but never felt a soul-deep gratification like he experienced with Sam. It was as if an invisible cord linked them, him feeding from her pleasure, his existence dependent on him taking her higher and higher.

However, that euphoric moment was over, and a thick cloud of confusion and uncertainty gathered around her as he paced the room. His gaze dropped to the nightstand, and he paused mid-stride, hands planted on his hips, staring at his crumpled business card, trying to figure out how it got there.

She pulled one of the flannel-covered pillows to her chest and said, "Wade gave me your card, but it got bent in my pocket."

Something about her defensiveness seemed off, but he didn't have room in his overtaxed brain to figure out the problem. His priority right now was to get his head straightened out before he ruined this time with her.

Time and space and running laps weren't going to change anything, and waiting two weeks to take their relationship to the next level was no longer an option.

He regretted things happening this way, but Sam already meant too much to him, and he refused to halt things now, which would be the same as turning away from her. Her insecurity sounded like an alarm, and he needed to silence it. Now.

He stretched out beside her, wrapped his palm around her jaw, and planted a slow, sensual kiss on her sweet, pink lips. "You're so incredibly beautiful, you drive me crazy. I needed a second to get myself under control. I'm sorry if I made you worry."

Before she had time to respond, he kissed her again. Only this time, he kissed her like the continuation of the human race depended on her understanding how badly he wanted her. He stroked her mouth and cajoled simmering responses from her, while her tongue danced and collided with his. He took his time simultaneously fucking and making love to her mouth, giving her a glimpse of what the rest of the night would bring.

She skimmed her trembling hands across his lower back, then pushed his shirt up and over his head. Sliding her hands around to his chest, she pressed against the front of his shoulders, pushing him backward. "I want you completely naked."

Happy to let her be in control for a while, he rolled onto his back and let her do things her way. With swift efficiency, she freed the button and zipper on his pants. Seconds later, his pants and boxer briefs joined his shirt on the floor, leaving him bare-ass naked and fully erect.

She brushed a tendril of hair from her face and crawled up his chest, then began a ravenous descent along his neck, over his clavicle, and down his torso. He hissed and stroked the back of her head as nerve endings came alive, all fighting and begging for a turn at being caressed by her tongue. She lavished his nipples with nips and sucks, then nibbled her way down his ribs to his abs. At this rate, she would eat him alive… And damn if he didn't want to give her a knife and fork to finish him off.

He vaguely remembered a concern about breaking her during rough sex, but if this were any indication, his fear had been unfounded. Nothing about her was meek or mild, and a tendril of fear that she might be like Lizbeth snaked along his spine.

However, as he finished the thought, she surprised him again by slowing her progress and becoming gentle, almost reverent in her touch as she reached his cock. His heart tripled its efforts and his lungs worked overtime to keep up with the extra stress on his body when she wrapped one hand under his balls, the other around his dick, and ran her tongue from base to sensitive tip. His hips kicked, his back arched, and he groaned in response.

"Damn, that's good."

A smile played at her lips as she moistened them before opening wide and sliding down his cock, taking him deep. Seeing her pink lips stretched around him made his brain stutter. When she flipped her lids wide and locked gazes with him while stroking up and down, his mind blipped and fizzled, then went completely blank.

With her body stretched out along the length of his, the only thing accessible to him was the top of her head. Even if he could reach the rest of her, she was still clothed, leaving him nothing to play with.

"Time for you to lose those clothes." He checked their position on the bed. "Will your ankle be all right off the side of the bed?"

She released him with a pop and licked her lips. "I think I'll survive."

For the second time today, she stripped off her T-shirt and shorts with the skill of a seasoned professional, although her bravado waned as she fumbled with the tie of her bathing suit.

Always the gentleman willing to give a hand, he untied the strings, then sat back and watched the panels of her top fall away.

Her large, dusky nipples tightened into tight peaks, taunting him, daring him to taste. He eased forward and took the closest into his mouth, then clamped his teeth over the bud and tugged. A deep moan emanated from her chest as she grabbed his head and held him in place. He tasted and teased until satisfied he'd had enough, at least for now, then eased onto his back.

"You're not finished undressing."

When she lay back on the bed and wiggled out of her bathing suit bottoms, it took everything in him to lay still and not dive on top of her, first with his mouth, then with his dick.

Sensing his impatience, she scrambled to her knees and shook her head. "Uh-uh, I'm playing right now."

"Correction: we're playing. Get up on all fours and turn that ass around here." He held his hand out, showing her exactly where he wanted her positioned.

Temporarily forgetting about the ankle, she slid around to form a ninety-degree angle with him. When she bumped her foot on the bed, she flinched and hissed with pain.

"Are you okay?"

She narrowed her eyes, acting playfully hostile. "I'm fine. Quit being such a worrywart."

He glared back and popped her bare ass. "Don't sass me."

"I will if I want." Mischief shimmered in her eyes as she wiggled her ass. "What are you gonna do about it?"

"Let me guess… You want more?" He laughed at her sheepish grin and ran his hand along the back of her thighs and over the curve of her ass. "I think this might be the perfect arrangement. I can spank you; you can suck me off."

Her eyes widened, then grew heavy lidded as she drew in a ragged breath. She started off running her tongue along the underside, like a cat lapping up cream, then varied her technique, mixing long, languorous strokes with short nips and shallow sucks.

When his first blow landed across her bare ass, she lifted her head and arched her back. With her eyes half-closed, her blond hair falling down her back and around her shoulders, she was a stunning picture of eroticism. But that wasn't how this was going to work, so he shook his head and gave her a warning look.

"If you stop, so will I."

She narrowed her eyes and exhaled roughly, but quickly surrendered to following his rules. He waited until she slid down his entire length and had her mouth filled before delivering another slap, this one sharper than the last. She sucked in a harsh breath through her nose and her body stiffened as she battled the urge to stop and cry out. Instead, she flattened her tongue and stroked him with more gusto than before and he rewarded her by spanking her pink-tinged ass.

He ran his hand over her pussy and thigh, not surprised to find the evidence of her excitement running down her leg. He slid two fingers into her and pumped in concert with her fucking him with her mouth. All too soon, he was at the verge of losing the load that had been building all day, and in a move that surprised even him, he said, "You're going to take every last drop, aren't you?"

Her nostrils flared, then her breathing stopped, as if thinking it over. A second later, she nodded and continued. He'd never demanded a lover finish him like this, but tonight he was consumed with the need to have Sam take all of him. Something in the back of his mind refused to accept she might reject him in any way.

He alternated slaps across her ass with finger-fucking her, and as her orgasm built, she jerked and tightened her lips around his cock, sweeping him away with his own. Throughout her climax, she continued to work him, drawing his release out until he became too sensitive to touch.

"No more." He gasped, grabbing her wrists and dragging her up so they were face to face. He wrapped his hands around the back of her neck and kissed her like she was the last breath of air he'd ever get.

When he regained some semblance of control, he scooted over and made room for her next to him. "I was supposed to be getting you a pillow and some ice."

She laughed and fluffed the pillow under her head. "The pillow is taken care of." Her eyes shifted and pink colored her cheeks. "We can skip the ice."

He tweaked her nipple and thought of the clamps he'd seen in the drawer. How many of those items could he use on her in one night? "Are you talking about ice for your foot or for another purpose?"

"My foot's fine." She shivered and made a funny face. "As for the other... I don't find ice erotic at all."

He cupped her breast in his palm and stroked his thumb over the nipple, coaxing the bud to harden. He dipped his head and licked the peak, then blew air across the moist skin, causing it to tighten even more. "Maybe whoever used it didn't do it right."

Her lids dipped and she bit her bottom lip. "Probably."

When she reached for the edge of the blanket to cover herself, he saw the action as a way of hiding, rather than her being cold. He took her hand in his and nipped her fingers.

"Who used the ice on you?"

Her eyebrows furrowed and her mouth tightened. "It doesn't matter. I don't like it."

He kissed her palm and studied her face, wondering why the subject made her so uncomfortable. He wanted to know what made her tick and was curious about her past. He was a man with a large ego and needed to make sure each experience with him was better than any she had before. But he mostly wanted to know how much experimentation she'd be willing to try. Based on the amount and variety of equipment in the drawer, he believed she'd be up for just about anything.

Using the firm voice he'd learned from Lucas, he said, "Tell me about your previous experience."

She swallowed and looked across the room. "I tried it by myself once."

The answer was so soft and strained he struggled to hear. Recognizing the response had cost her dearly, he rewarded her with a long, slow kiss.

He stroked her hipbone and up to her breast. "Would you be willing to try again, if I promise to stop if you ask me to?"

"Why?" she asked, wariness heavy in her eyes and voice.

He shrugged and brushed her arm. "You have a drawer full of interesting toys. I figure you must be pretty adventurous. Ice can be an interesting addition."

The wariness lingered, along with a flash of something else. "You've used it before." It wasn't a question, but a statement… one he chose to leave unanswered.

"Tell me about the double dildo."

She was shaking her head no before he even finished the sentence.

He laughed and cupped her cheek, holding her head and gaze steady. "Yes."

"You don't need to know everything."

"I need to know if you can take both of them, because if you can…" He let the sentence die off, allowing her to interpret the implication.

She gulped once, then again, struggling for breath. But he didn't let go of her face or allow her to look away.

Finally relenting, she whispered, "Yes. I can take both of them." Her voice grew stronger and more defiant as she finished the sentence with an implied, *Are you happy now?*

He grinned and kissed the tip of her nose. *Yep, I'm very happy.* In fact, he was ecstatic. Which was very strange, considering he hadn't even made love to her yet—at least, not technically.

He eased against the headboard and pulled her with him, wrapping her tightly in his arms, holding her close while his body prepared for the next round.

As the creak in the bed silenced, he caught the vibration in his pant pocket, which zapped his happy and ushered in a truckload of guilt. He didn't regret anything that happened so far, or what would happen for the remainder of the night. He did, however, regret not ending things with Lizbeth sooner.

He couldn't go back three or four months, nor could he take back last night. He couldn't change anything about today or what just happened in this bedroom.

He could do things differently over the next several days, but he wouldn't. He had what he wanted in his arms, and he refused to let go for any reason.

As he drew in a deep breath and nuzzled Sam closer, his conscience snorted and said, *And everyone thinks you're such a nice guy.*

Chapter Twelve

*H*ad Sam not aced biology, she would've thought a nerve ran from Kevin's skeletal system to his cell phone. When the vibrating stopped, his arms around her relaxed and his breathing eased. When the vibration resumed, his arms flexed, his body snapped tight, and his breath came in sharp, shallow punches.

She pushed against his chest, preparing to move off him, but his grip tightened.

"Where are you going?"

"Don't you want to get your phone?"

His neck worked back and forth in an attempt to shake his head no. "They'll leave a message if it's important."

"It's rung three times in two minutes. What if it's Marianne?"

The corner of his mouth kicked up in a smirk... or maybe a grimace. "It's not Marianne." He pressed his lips to hers in a long, lingering and extremely persuasive kiss. "Don't give my phone another thought."

Well, when he put it like that, who was she to argue?

"Okay." She relaxed into his side with a sigh. "If you're not worried, I guess I shouldn't be." She drew in a deep breath and enjoyed his heady, male scent as she brushed her fingers through his curly chest hair.

He closed his eyes and a hiss pushed through his lips as she stroked the tip of her short nail over his nipple.

"I had plans for those toys… still do, eventually." He slid his hand under her ass and lifted, rolling her over on top of him. "But tonight, I like the idea of figuring you out without any extraneous equipment. Just me and your body." He cupped her face and kissed the tip of her nose before moving on to her forehead and temple and lips.

As he took his time exploring her body, a fire grew in the pit of her stomach, making her squirm and shimmy up his waist, trying to get his growing erection where she wanted it most.

"You're not supposed to be this slow and patient. You're supposed to be a rip-and-strip kind of guy."

He laughed in a short burst. "A what?"

"You know, no patience, no foreplay, just rip and strip."

His brow creased in a mixture of confusion and amusement. "Foreplay is half the fun. Why would you think I'd skip that?"

"Never mind." She wiggled some more, trying to fit the pieces together. "Are you gonna do this or what?"

His eyes smiled. "I need to grab those condoms from the drawer first."

Anxious to move things along, she scrambled off him and enjoyed the view of his heavily muscled ass and thighs as he strode to her dresser. He retrieved the box from the drawer and tossed it in the air as he walked back to the bed, grinning. "This should take care of us for tonight. I'll buy replacements tomorrow."

His long, powerful strides and predatory gleam sent a shiver of anticipation snaking down her spine and wrapping around her belly. His erection made a full reappearance and the memory of taking him, as well as his taste lingering on her tongue, had her licking her lips and swallowing harshly.

She'd only finished Michael like that one time, and the memory wasn't a fond one. But with Kevin, she hadn't been given much of a choice—although, she suspected if she objected, he would've let her up. But his commanding tone, along with the fear of rejection she'd caught in his eyes, made her eager to take all of him.

"You're looking at me like I'd make a great midnight snack. Didn't you get enough earlier?"

She gnawed on her lip and dipped her head to hide the blush. "Apparently not."

"I'll be happy to feed you anytime you're hungry," he murmured, sitting on the edge of the bed, using his finger to brush a stray hair from her face before running it along her neck in a light, sweeping stroke. "All you have to do is ask."

"Is that what you're bringing for breakfast Monday? Wade might object."

He laughed and kissed her jaw, then nipped at her ear. "Maybe lunch." He paused and sighed. "I won't be here for lunch Monday." His eyes were shadowed as his gaze settled on her face. "I hope to be back in time for dinner, though. Will you be free?"

Dinner on Monday would have them together three days in a row, and concern over spending so much time with him tugged at the back of her mind. She was especially concerned about Michy getting the wrong idea or forming too close an attachment.

However, thoughts of worry or fear, along with all the reasons it would be a bad idea, promptly fled when he took a foil pack from the box, tossed the carton onto the nightstand, and gripped his straining erection. He stood at the side of the bed and rolled the condom on while gazing down at her.

"Scoot over here."

He slid his hands under her butt and settled her at the edge of the bed, perfectly aligned for him to enter her. With his hands under her knees, he supported her legs, making sure her ankle was clear, and drove into her with one long, fluid stroke.

She cried out at the sharp invasion, then moaned with pleasure when he didn't stop to give her time to adjust, but eased out and drove back in. The third time he paused, giving her a moment to appreciate being completely filled.

He closed his eyes, dropped his head back, and rocked his hips in slow, languorous strokes. The way his shoulders rolled and his abs contracted while his hips and thighs flexed reminded her of a lava lamp.

There was nothing sharp or forced about his movements… just a continual ebb and flow of motion as he joined their bodies, then rolled out before rocking in again. The beauty and fluidity of his motions, as well as the concentration on his face as he thrust and retreated, hypnotized her. When he dropped his gaze to hers, the soft gooiness in his eyes and the sensual smile on his full lips filled her chest with warmth.

Boy, had she ever been wrong in her expectations. He did know how to be patient and slow… maddeningly slow. She arched her back and thrust her hips upward, needing to be closer, but he had a different plan in mind. He eased out until the tip of his cock hovered at her entrance, then dipped to the side so her left ankle settled on his shoulder. He gripped his cock in his hand and used the tip to stroke back and forth over her clit, like flicking bunny ears, only a million times better.

Within seconds, the extra stimulation had her bucking and inching closer, trying to get a stronger, firmer contact. "Oh God, that's good. More. More."

He laughed and flicked a few more times before settling back into her. "Anyone ever tell you you're a greedy lover?"

Even though he was teasing and there wasn't anything offensive about his comment, the question stopped her cold. No, no one had ever accused her of being greedy in bed. In fact, she'd only had a few lovers prior to Michael and they hadn't been anything exceptional. Then came Michael, and while the sex was okay in the beginning, it was never spectacular.

Michaela was born, her dad died, her stress levels shot through the roof, and her sex drive crashed. The result had been him declaring her cold and uninterested, not only in him, but in sex altogether. He found someone else, and she found a magazine full of adult toys. So no, no one had ever driven her wild and made her beg for more.

"Hey." Kevin's gentle voice brought her back to the present. He pushed all the way in and leaned forward, settling his face close to hers. "Where'd you go?"

"Nowhere." She shook her head and tried to smile. "I'm right here. You feel *so good.*" She emphasized *so* and *good,* making them porn star worthy in hopes of selling her story, but fell seriously short of the mark.

His eyebrow shot up into an *oh really* arch. "Wanna try again?"

"No." She ran her fingertips over the soft skin covering his hard shoulders and magnificent chest. "Seriously, I'm right here, and you do feel amazing." She fought the need clawing at her chest to wrap her arms around him and draw him close to her heart.

Physically feeling good during sex was expected. Incorporating emotions was dangerous and she refused to allow them in. She didn't want to think about how sweet he'd been to her and Michy or how concerned he'd been about her ankle and how hard he worked to make her comfortable.

She ignored the tug in her chest and the squishiness in her belly and switched her focus to a more important, or at least more pertinent, topic. "It's especially good when you do that thing you did a minute ago." She thrust her hips forward and wiggled encouragingly. "Will you do it again?"

He worked his mouth like he wanted to call "bullshit," and his eyes remained guarded and unconvinced, but he let her off the hook and took his cock in hand. "This thing?"

"Oh yeah." She arched her back off the mattress. "That's not just good; it's freakin' fantastic."

He rested his elbow on the bed so his other hand was free and tweaked her nipple while continuing to work her clit. She kept her left foot free and clear, but wrapped her right leg around his back and dug her heel into his ass, then worked his nipple too.

His eyes and nostrils flared and the sweet gooiness that previously oozed off him melted away, exposing a raw, powerful male. He pushed into her and the slow, languid movements became powerful, driving thrusts. His concentration returned, but this time, rather than focusing on sensuous, rhythmic movements, he focused on driving them off a cliff.

When he pinched her clit and tilted up, leveraging his thrust against her G-spot, nirvana rushed in and swept her away. Seconds later, he caught the wave with her. His neck muscles tightened and strained as he threw his head back and a groan rose from his chest.

She'd never seen anything as magnificent as him in the throes of an orgasm… And she already couldn't wait to do it again.

Sam was insatiable. Not that Kevin was complaining.

She was full of passion and fire, and every time he was ready to go, she was right there with him. Sometime between two and three, he'd fallen asleep with her wrapped in his arms, her head resting on his chest.

He hadn't needed a beer. He hadn't wanted a shot. He was as content as ever, and sleep came swiftly and easily.

He drifted awake to a rain of sweet, gentle kisses on his chest. When he rocked his head to the side and looked at her through hooded eyes, she gave him a sleepy little smile, then rolled over and wiggled closer, pressing her ass against his side.

He rolled with her so they were perfectly aligned, like spoons in a drawer, and ran his hand from the swell of her breast down the indentation of her waist to her hipbone. "You ready for more, sugar?"

"Where you're concerned, I'm always ready for more." She arched her back and pressed her ass firmly against his hardening cock.

So far, with the exception of the initial spanking, things remained traditional. He wasn't sure if there was a hint behind the ass-to-cock business, but figured this was as good a time as any to step things up a notch and see how far she'd be willing to go. His hope was, in a super-sexed state, she'd let her guard down and answer questions more freely than earlier, when he'd accidentally stumbled across her toy box—which shocked the shit out of them both.

He lifted her top leg over his, opening her to him, then ran his hand under the soft curve of her butt to her slick and ready-again sex.

"I'm going to start calling you More."

She gave a husky laugh and reached backward between their bodies for his cock. Stroking and squeezing, she guided him to her. "As long as you back it up with action, I won't mind."

He laughed at her impatience. "Not yet, *amore mio*."

He slipped two fingers into her, temporarily satisfying her, then dragged the juices from her pussy back toward her ass. She froze and her breathing stuttered, but she didn't stop him or move away.

"Is this what you're trying to tell me you want with all the ass grinding and wiggling?"

Her only response, besides another little wiggle, was an uncomfortable choking cough. Taking that as a consensual invitation, if not a yes, he gathered more lubrication and worked his ring finger into her tight opening. His finger was nothing in comparison to the double-dildo, and she sighed as her muscles relaxed, accepting the invasion.

Shit, that double dick had been a major surprise, especially when her eyes went straight to it when he asked about her favorite toy.

Was she into threesomes?

If so, could he share?

The thought dropped a chunk of cold dread in his chest like a block of ice. He'd shared women with Steve in college. Lizbeth had even suggested bringing in another playmate at one time; something he'd been willing to try if they'd found the right person. But the idea of sharing Sam held no appeal.

"Have you been with two guys at once?"

"No." She shook her head and moaned again, then arched her body into a C, pressing her backside into him as he penetrated her farther, then worked his finger in a circle, stretching her.

"Do you want to be with two men?" The question came out more as a growl than a general question, but he couldn't help himself. The whole idea left him nauseous.

He was fully aware of the double-standard flag waving around his head, but he didn't give a shit. Her failure to answer unnerved him, so he dropped back and punted, easing into the discussion with something he already knew.

"You said you use the double dildo."

"Yes," she answered raggedly.

He stretched his free arm out from under her and took hold of her wrist, pinning her in place. "Have you had anal sex with a man?"

"No." Her breath came in short, shallow gasps and her pulse

pounded against his palm.

"But you want to." He posed it as a statement, rather than a question, but she answered anyway.

"Sometime. Yes."

Sometime. Not now.

"Do you like being held down?" His voice was so thick it sounded like his throat had been glued together with flypaper.

Her shoulder shifted in a shrug, her ass grinded against his finger, and she moaned low in her throat. All solid indicators of a *hell yeah*, but she said, "I don't know."

"Yes, you do know. You may not have been tied down before, but I'm holding you now. Do you like it?"

She squirmed under him, not in an attempt to get away, but in an attempt to get closer, to angle her body with his so he could penetrate her. He removed his finger from her ass and obliged her by guiding his cock to her opening. However, before he gave her what she wanted, he would get an answer.

"I'm still waiting. Do you like being held down?"

"Yes, dammit. Now fuck me."

He eased into her, but still not to the extent she wanted. Obsessing over the threesome thing would drive him batshit crazy if he didn't find out exactly where she stood on the subject. He ran his hand along her jaw, then forced his thumb between her parted lips.

She clamped down and circled her tongue over and around, then nipped at the skin on the pad of this thumb.

"Do you want two men doing you at the same time, Sam? Do you want one man fucking you while you suck the other off? Or do you want two men fucking you at once—one in your pussy, one in your ass?"

She gasped for air while trying to maintain the suction on his thumb. Her left hand grabbed his arm, holding his thumb in place, while the other wrapped over his side and grabbed his ass, urging him to drive into her.

Shit, whether she wanted it or not, talking about a threesome was driving her wild, and she was on the verge of coming without him completely penetrating her.

That's when he realized he wasn't wearing a condom. He didn't know if Sam was on the pill, and even if she was, he wouldn't risk coming in her unprotected. He gritted his teeth to keep hold of his control, used his free hand to work her clit, and got down and dirty with the sexy talk.

A second later she exploded in his arms, coming in wave after wave after wave. He rolled her onto her stomach, took his cock into his hand, and came in heavy bursts on her back. When he finished, he flopped down beside her and gasped.

"No condom. Are you on the pill?"

Still trembling from her orgasm, she nodded and said, "Yeah, it's okay." She pegged him with a hard stare. "Next time, don't cheat me."

After wiping her off, he collapsed onto the bed and snuggled her close. They'd already talked about him moving to the couch before Michaela woke up, but he wasn't ready to leave the warm bed or the warm body curled next to him.

While she played with the hair on his chest, she drew in a deep breath, opened her mouth to speak, then closed it with a sigh.

"Whatever's on your mind, spit it out."

After a few more starts and stops, she quietly said, "I like the fantasy of being with two guys, but I'm not sure I'd like the reality."

His breath left in a whoosh as relief rushed through him. He tilted his head so he could look her in the eyes and said, "I can make the fantasy very real. But I don't think I could share you."

Her smile was as bright as the rising sun as she stretched up to kiss him. "Can you manage to be three or four guys yourself?"

He laughed and slapped her ass. "Your new name is definitely More."

Chapter Thirteen

*W*hen Sam woke Sunday morning, she had a difficult time getting the fragmented pieces of her brain to mesh together. The sheets were tangled around her body, her ankle throbbed, her muscles were sore from neck to thigh, and her room smelled like sex.

Memories of the previous night seeped into her consciousness and had her grabbing the spare pillow. A deep breath confirmed she wasn't dreaming; the flannel carried Kevin's scent, and his deep, male voice rumbled in the distance. He spoke again and Michaela giggled as the mouth-watering aroma of bacon drifted under the closed door.

She rolled over and checked the clock. *Holy shit!* With a start, she jerked upright, then regretted the sudden movement, as all of her muscles snapped to attention, reminding her of the extreme workout they'd received over the past twelve hours. She hadn't slept until ten o'clock since Michaela was born, but after the sexual marathon she and Kevin ran last night, she was grateful for the rest.

She untangled from the sheets and slung her legs over the side of the bed. Her ankle was an ugly mixture of black and green and swollen, and protested to the nth degree when she tried to settle weight on it. She dropped back down to the bed and sighed. Last evening, Kevin suggested crutches, but she'd refused. The idea of him taking care of her was infinitely more appealing than hobbling around on sticks, but she needed to do something so she could get around at work.

Giving up on walking, she kept her foot suspended and hopped to the dresser where she grabbed a pair of sweats and a T-shirt. She needed a shower before she dressed for the day, but she wanted to speak to Kevin and Michaela and let them know she was awake.

As she hobbled down the hall, the pair's voices bubbled from the kitchen as they talked like they'd known each other forever. Sam stopped at the doorway and watched Kevin pour batter into the skillet, while Michaela stood on the stool next to him, spatula at the ready.

"Wait until they bubble before you try and turn them," Kevin said, setting the glass mixing bowl on the counter.

The two of them stood side by side, lost to their own thoughts, waiting for the bubbles to appear. Michael wasn't an overly tolerant man, and his lack of patience had never been more obvious than when dealing with his daughter. Sam crossed her arms to assuage the pain squeezing her chest as she was again struck with the painful awareness of how much Michy had missed out on, even while living in the same house as her father.

She was also faced with the glaring truth of how badly she misread Kevin at the jobsite. He had patience in spades last night, and now, he seemed perfectly content to stand with Michy like nothing was more important than making pancakes.

The problem was Kevin wasn't a permanent fixture in their lives and she didn't want Michaela to get attached, only to have him disappear like her papa and father.

You should follow your own advice, chica. You seem to be getting awfully attached yourself.

"Look, they're bubbling," Michy said, a big smile on her face as she pointed to the pancakes and jumped up and down on the chair.

"Whoa, *folletta*, be careful," he said, wrapping a protective arm around her. "Don't dump yourself off that chair."

Michy flashed her too-cute-for-her-own-damned-good grin. "That's why Mommy doesn't want me standing on the chairs to fix my own food. She lets me make mud pies outside, but I don't get to cook inside."

Kevin's eyes went wide. "Uh-oh." He leaned close and lowered his voice. "We better not tell her about this."

"Too late."

Sam laughed as their heads snapped around, GUILTY stamped all over their expressions. Michy maintained the mouth-wide-open stare, but Kevin quickly recovered. He raised an eyebrow and tilted his head toward Michy, his question obvious.

Sam waved off his concern. "You guys can finish." She met Kevin's stare and smiled softly. "Thanks for letting me sleep late and for fixing breakfast."

His wink was intimate and carried the weight of a physical touch. "You're welcome. I thought maybe you could use the rest."

"Thanks, Mommy." Looking at Kevin with wide, adoring eyes, she said, "Now?"

"Yeah, *folletta,* go ahead."

Michy's smile grew wide and her chest puffed out proudly. Looking at Sam over her shoulder, she said, "Kevin said I can be the pixie since I'm the littlest." She turned back to the stove and with deep concentration, stuck her tongue out, and slid the spatula under the pancake.

Kevin held his breath, watching and waiting while she carefully flipped it over. "Good job," he said, taking a deep breath and smiling proudly as they high-fived. "You've gotten good at this. We're gonna make you the official pancake cooker." He cut his eyes to Sam. "Once you're big enough to do it without standing on the chair."

"Or when you're with me," she said.

Kevin's gaze followed Sam as she hopped to the counter and

snagged a piece of bacon. "Not any better today, huh?"

She scrunched up her face in disappointment and shook her head. "I may need to break down and get some crutches." She rolled her eyes at him. "Like someone suggested yesterday."

"You don't need those, Mommy," Michy said after flipping the second pancake. "Me and Kevin can take care of you." She turned to him for confirmation. "Right?"

"Yeah, we can probably handle that. At least today"—he shifted his darkening gaze to Sam—"and tonight. But tomorrow you'll be in school, I'll be in Riverside, and she has to work. What's she gonna do without our help?"

Michy thought while she flipped the third pancake, then shrugged. "I guess she needs trutches."

Sam took a seat at the kitchen table while the dynamic duo finished the pancakes and set the table, serving up crispy bacon and glasses of orange juice. Kevin helped Michy climb into her chair and had just settled in his seat when his phone started vibrating again.

The muscle in his jaw ticked and he gave a slight huff, though Sam had the distinct impression he tried not to show any reaction.

She reached across the table and took his hand as he reached for a piece of bacon. "Someone's trying awfully hard to get in touch with you. Why don't you answer?" When he winced and shook his head, she released his hand and leaned back in her chair. "Is it Lizilla?"

He jerked back, shock lighting up his face. "How do you know about her?"

"Wade told me. He said in the process of helping with his wedding, you'd gotten strapped with a problematic sister of the bride." She grabbed a pancake from the stack and slathered on a generous portion of butter.

He swallowed a gulp of orange juice and carefully set the glass on the table. "What else did he tell you?"

"That's about it." She grinned. "I tried to imagine you in the typical wedding director clothing: sundress, white gloves, maybe a large hat. I couldn't make the image fly, though." She cut her pancake and took a bite. "Is that who keeps calling? Who was calling last night?"

He chewed a bite of bacon and took another drink of orange juice. "Yeah." His voice was low, sad.

"What's wrong?" She set her fork down and rested her hand on his. "Is there a problem with the wedding?"

"No." He slipped his hand out from under hers, leaned back in his chair, and pushed his plate away. "There's no problem with the wedding." He glanced at Sam before staring out the window, a pained expression crumpling his forehead.

"Don't you like your pancakes?" Michy's small voice cut through the tension in the room.

His attention snapped to her and a wide, genuine smile erased the despair straining his features. "I love the pancakes. They're the best I've ever had." He took a deep breath and pulled his plate to the edge of the table. To Sam, he said, "I'll call her later. Right now, I have a stack of pancakes to eat."

While Sam took a shower and Michaela watched a repeat performance of *Beauty and the Beast,* Kevin stepped out onto the backyard patio with his cell. He wished he'd saved himself a whole lot of stress, guilt, and shame by turning the damned thing off, but he always kept it on in case Marianne needed him.

Last check, he had six missed calls, all from Lizbeth, and three messages. Without bothering to listen to voicemail, he pulled up her number and braced himself for a conversation he had no idea how to handle.

As he watched shadows from the neighbor's tree dance across the small backyard, he laid out his plan. Hopefully, a brief conversation would satisfy Lizbeth for the remainder of the day, thereby preventing further phone calls. Then, tomorrow morning, he'd go to Riverside and officially end things.

Out of time and options, he leaned against the back wall of Sam's house and hit call.

Lizbeth answered on the first ring, panic coloring her voice. "I've been worried sick about you. Why haven't you been answering?"

Kevin banged his head against the back of the house and took a deep breath. Unless he ended the relationship now—and ending a long-term relationship over the phone was cruel by any standards—the only safe way out of this conversation would be to straight-up lie. He hated going that route, but didn't see any other choice.

He took a deep breath and said, "Sorry, I've been tied up. You know, work stuff." That should put a quick end to the questions. "I haven't listened to your messages yet. What's going on?"

He peered around the edge of the house, through the slider, and into the living room, making sure the Beast was still on the job, keeping Michaela entertained.

Admittedly, he also wanted to confirm the living room was free and clear of Sam.

"We have a problem with the caterer and now, on top of everything else, they're talking about a possible storm."

He worked his neck in a circle and took a deep breath. "Lizbeth, it's the middle of September, the peak of hurricane season. We knew going in we faced the risk of a storm, which is why we developed the contingency plan with Kat and Erik and arranged to use their house and guesthouse if necessary. You're talking two weeks out. The forecasters can't predict what's going to happen that far in advance."

"But they say all the models are calling for a storm to form in the Atlantic."

Her whine reached jet engine proportions and while he prided himself on being reasonable and patient, kind and understanding, it all dried up and blew away in a flash. He felt like the prospective hurricane roared through his system and ripped his decency to shreds, leaving him without a sliver of compassion.

"Lizbeth, this is absurd. The wedding is in two fucking weeks. How in God's name do you expect anyone to know what's going to happen with the weather this far in advance? They can't even get tomorrow right. We have a contingency plan in place in case the weather gets bad. What the fuck do you want from me?"

He pushed his hands through his hair, shoved off the wall, and turned toward the house… At the same instant, Sam froze with her hand on the glass slider handle. Her mouth fell open, her eyes widened, and she didn't even appear to be breathing, as if any sudden movement might provoke his wrath upon her too.

Lizbeth sniffed on the other end of the line and he had the sense real tears were being shed. "I know it's crazy, but I want my baby sister's wedding to be perfect. Please tell me everything's all right."

She might've been talking solely about the wedding, but something in her tone made him think she recognized his explosion was about more than caterers and the weather. She obviously needed reassurances for something, but the answer was the same on all accounts, and he couldn't make her any guarantees.

With his gaze still locked onto Sam's, he gripped the phone so hard his hand ached. "I need to go right now, but I'm coming to Riverside first thing in the morning. Be available. We need to talk."

Without waiting for her reply, he disconnected the call and inched his way toward the door. He tried to think about the entire conversation, to remember what he'd said so he could figure out what Sam might've overheard. But he was so angry with Lizbeth and furious for getting himself into this situation, he couldn't settle his mind enough to think.

As he approached the door, Sam stepped to the side, making room for him to enter. The bright sunlight gave her eyes a bluish-green cast, making them even more beautiful than before. They were filled with concern that he didn't deserve, and he found himself unable to look at her.

"Is everything okay?" she asked softly as he slid the door closed.

If anything he said gave the impression Lizbeth was more than a troublesome sister-of-the bride, he had to believe Sam would be looking for space on the wall to hang his head, not showing concern.

Somehow, over the past forty-eight hours, he'd gone from praying for strength to get through two more weeks to praying for the grace of one more day.

Just one more day and he'd be free of his obligation to Lizbeth. He could pursue this thing with Sam without guilt and shame weighing him down, or fear of the truth revealing itself looming over his head.

"Yeah," he said, trying to sound as convincing as possible. "Everything's fine."

He wrapped his arm around her waist and helped her hobble across the living room to the sofa, where he sat next to Michy, pulling Sam into his lap. "Who wants to go swimming?"

"Meeeeeee!" Michaela sprang off the couch like a jack-in-the-box and took off toward her bedroom, presumably in search of a bathing suit.

"Do you ever skinny dip in that pool?" Sam asked, wrapping her arms around his neck and whispering in his ear.

He laughed and shook his head. "No, I've never had a reason to. But I bet I can get Marianne to keep Michaela one night this week…"

Chapter Fourteen

*W*ith Kevin going to Riverside on Monday to deal with wedding stuff, Sam wanted to go ahead and run her ideas by him, giving him time to digest them tonight and maybe make some decisions while driving the next day. Her ability to help him was limited and only possible after he obtained a revised site plan—which couldn't be done until he made a decision on the best way to solve the problem.

Their first order of business was swimming with the kids—mostly Kevin swam while she sat on the side of the pool and stayed out of the way. Then they'd get to work.

"Uncle Kevin, throw me in again. Pleeeease."

"Me, too. Me, too."

"One last time," Kevin said, putting on a fabulous show of flexing arms and back muscles as he pulled himself out of the pool. His body was a work of art, without an ounce of fat to be found—something she'd verified with hours of visual and physical inspection.

She sighed at his beauty as he walked toward her... then hovered over her and shook like a dog.

"Gee, thanks." She wiped a stream of water from her face. "That's all right. I was starting to get hot anyway."

He bent down on one knee, leaned over her shoulder, and held her chin in his fingers while giving her a smooth, languorous kiss. "You're always hot."

With a smile and a wink that left her belly fluttering, he walked to the deep end where the kids stood shivering in the shade, waiting for another toss-in. "This is the last one. Sam and I have a little work to do." He paused, then looked up at her and smiled as if he liked the way that sounded.

She liked the sound of it too, for several reasons. She loved this type of work and desperately wanted to get back to the building side of things, rather than doing inspections for the rest of her life. Anytime she had the opportunity to talk over the development phase of a project, she would jump.

She and her daddy talked shop all the time, something her mother and brothers often complained about. They didn't understand something always needed to be worked through, and it was easy for Sam and her father to jump into conversation about a project while sitting around watching football, or even during family dinners.

Sam also liked having a man in her life with whom she could share project logistics. Michael could've cared less about her work, since he didn't want her working in the first place, so he'd never been interested—

Why in the world was she thinking things like *a man in her life?* She didn't want a man in her life. Kevin was a temporary thing… like a new toy for her collection. Only this toy breathed and kissed and moved independently, and boy, did he ever move. He had moves she couldn't ever dream up, and even if she did, she'd never be able to make those vibrating pieces of plastic feel so friggin' fantastic. But that didn't make him anything more than a temporary good time, and she'd be well served to remember that.

"Okay, that's it for now," Kevin said as Spencer popped up from the water. "We'll be sitting at the patio table, working, but we can still see you guys. All right?"

Grumbled "yes, sirs" and "fines" came from the pool as Kevin grabbed his towel and ran it over his head and the back of his neck, then paused mid-swipe. Cocking his head to the side, he studied Sam for a moment, then sat down on a nearby chair.

"Hey," his soft and gentle tone tugged at her. "What's wrong? You hurting that bad?"

Shaking off the melancholy thoughts of her daddy and the way her life had been before, she said, "No, I'm fine." She grabbed her towel and dried her legs. "I have your job folder and the site plan in my bag. Do you mind grabbing them from the house?"

"Of course not. Do you want something to drink?"

Kevin had forgone the cooler today, but made several trips in and out of the house for water and lemonade. This seemed to be a new thing for him, and several times she'd caught him taking a drink of his water, then holding the bottle up and looking at it, as if surprised it tasted so good.

"A glass of sweet tea would be great."

He'd already started toward the house and stopped mid-stride to turn around. "Iced tea?"

She grinned and nodded. "Yeah, any Southern boy worth his salt will have sweet iced tea on hand."

His shoulders drooped as he slowly shook his head. "I guess I'm a total disappointment." He brightened. "At least this time. Next time, I won't let ya down."

As he disappeared into the house, she pushed to a standing position and began the slow, laborious, and extremely painful trek across the patio to the Holden's outdoor table that was so big it could accommodate an entire family reunion. She flopped down in the chair and propped her foot up on the seat next to her as Kevin exited the house.

He looked around the pool for her, and when he found her at the table, frowned. "Jesus, woman, you're the most stubborn person I've ever met."

"I'm not an invalid. You, yourself, pointed out I'm going to need to figure out a way to get around tomorrow." She shrugged. "Why not start now?"

He set her bag and two bottles of water on the table and leaned down nose to nose with her. "Someone needs another spanking."

Whoosh! Just like that, with a single sentence, a fire erupted in her belly and spread upward into her chest and breasts and down through her sex. *Yes, please,* was the only intelligible thought that came to mind, but she hadn't meant to actually say it. However, the words were out and she couldn't take them back, so she laughed and said, "My new name's More, remember?"

His eyes were like onyx, dark and soft, and his mouth gathered like it did when he was deep in thought. "I've been thinking about that *more* you seemed so interested in. I need to make a phone call, but I think I've figured out a way we can make your fantasy threesome happen."

Sam's heart rate hit triple time. "We?" she squeaked. "As in you and me or you and"—she gulped—"someone else?"

Although still dark with passion, his eyes softened, as did his features as he knelt in front of her. "I heard every word you said."

That was scary, because several times she'd been crazy out of her mind. She had no idea what all she said in her sexed-up state, but she got the impression, right now, he was strictly talking about her fantasy threesome. She'd been terrified of admitting the fantasy, but her answer seemed important. When he responded with great relief at hearing it was only a fantasy, she was glad she'd shared the private information.

His steady gaze locked onto hers and held her tight. Reaching for her hand, he said, "I know your boundaries. Will you trust me to fulfill your fantasy?"

He knew she wanted a threesome, but he also understood it needed to be a twosome, giving the impression of a threesome.

"Yes." Chill bumps rushed up her arms as she shook her head nervously. "I trust you."

"Thank you." He leaned in for a slow, bone-melting kiss before standing and pushing her bag over to her.

The heat of the moment dissipated on the breeze as Sam pulled out the Vanguard file and site map.

Kevin was all business as he scooted a chair around next to hers and said, "I can't tell you how much I appreciate you working on this for me the other night." He ran a hand over the top of his head and sighed. "This project has been my baby from the beginning. I was concerned about jumping the gun without the tower, but Papà convinced me it would be fine."

"Daddy and I had a similar situation once, which is why I felt I might be able to help." She rolled the site map out between them and pointed to where the water line came onto the property. "Right now, the water line goes to the box here"—she pointed to a location off to the left of the club house—"and then divides into the individual buildings."

She pulled out the tracing paper she'd used for drawing an alternative map and laid it over the site plan. "You're gonna have to run a new four-inch line from the road directly to the dumpster pad back here in the corner, build a small, temporary shelter for the booster pump, then route the water back to the cut-off. God willing, you'll never use the booster pump, so as soon as the tower's installed, you can resell the pump and remove the temporary shelter. Or, you can build the structure so the front wall stays intact and acts as a barrier to hide the dumpster."

She ran through a few other possible options, none of which were any less expensive than the first, and, in her opinion, none as good. They would all create additional work, like tearing up the parking lot and landscaping in multiple locations, rather than the few places she marked. Also, if they ever had a leak, it would be a nightmare to figure out where the problem originated.

Kevin listened to all of the options and studied the plan and her notes carefully. After several moments of silence, he leaned back in the chair, wrapped his arm around the back of hers, and said, "Personally, you prefer the first option, right?"

"Yeah, it's going to be a pain in the ass and expensive to run an additional water line from the road to the future pump house, but you'll only have to cut the pavement in..."—she counted the places they would need to cross the road and parking lot—"three places. And they're narrow trenches." She winced. "You'll need to do curb and gutter repair in two places, but I still think you'd be better off going this route than any of the others."

He rested his elbow on the armrest, propped his head in his hand, and stared at her. After a long, looooong uncomfortable silence, he said, "You're not only beautiful; you're smart."

Heat infused her face while her chest filled with pride. No one but her daddy ever acknowledged her competency on a job, and while the reminder sent a pang of sadness through her, she also sat a little taller. "Thanks. But, like I said, I've been through this, so the experience helps."

His eyes narrowed and his demeanor chilled. "Your brothers' lack of faith did a real head-job on you."

She laughed uncomfortably. "Yeah, of course. That and—" She cut off the thought, refusing to allow Michael to be a part of this conversation. "When someone doubts your ability, it messes with your head."

"It wasn't just someone, Sam, it was your whole family."

She drew in a breath and slowly exhaled, pushing the pain out with the air. "Yeah."

He leaned forward in the chair and took hold of her hand. "Their stupidity is gonna be my gain. Come to the office Tuesday morning and meet with Marianne and me." He grinned. "She's gonna have my ass for jumping the gun like this, but I don't need more research."

"If she needs more research to be comfortable with a decision, then she should do it. I can give you the name of another builder in Columbia who had a similar situation. He can tell you how he solved the issue." She grinned. "Although, he's going to tell you the same thing."

His grin broadened and his eyes sparkled. "You misunderstood what I was saying—"

A young, attractive brunette stepped onto the patio from the Holden home, interrupting his sentence. "Oh, I'm sorry." She jumped back a step, startled by their presence. "I didn't know you were over here. I'm sorry to interrupt."

"Hey, Callie, it's okay." He stood and greeted the young woman with a hug. "Come here. I want you to meet someone."

"Sam, this is Callie Holden. She's recently gone to work for us and will be responsible for decorating the Vanguard buildings"—he paused to playfully glare at Sam—"as soon as the mean building inspector gives me my CO. Callie, this is Sam Wallace… the mean building inspector who won't give me my CO."

Callie laughed as she shook Sam's hand. "She doesn't look mean to me."

Kevin snorted and crossed his arms over his chest while widening his stance. "Don't be fooled by the pretty face."

Sam laughed at his teasing and took a brief moment to enjoy the playful intimacy. Getting on board with the act, she crossed her arms in return, then threw him the bone she'd been holding on to. "After that comment, forget the temporary CO I'd planned to give you."

"What?" Kevin's arms fell to his sides while the rest of his body snapped to full alert. "You can do that?"

"Well…" She moved her head side to side. "Once I get the revised site plan back from the engineer, showing the proposed changes, I can walk it through permitting and get you a temporary CO. Only so Callie, and the other finishing contractors, can get in to set things up and prepare for opening. Not one customer is to set foot in that building."

Kevin squeezed his eyes shut and muttered something in Italian before kneeling in front of her and wrapping her in a hug so tight she could barely breath. "Thank you. Thank you…" His voice cracked and he buried his head in her neck. "You have no idea what a blessing you are. Thank you."

Callie cleared her throat and backed toward the door. "Okay, well, just give me a call when you're ready for me. Sam, it was nice to meet you."

He pushed to his feet and said, "I'll give you a call Tuesday or Wednesday and let you know where things stand."

As Callie disappeared into the house, he sat back down in his chair and faced Sam. "Sorry to chick out on you, I just…" He rubbed the back of his neck. "You've been such a pleasant surprise in my life."

He rested his forearms on the table and opened his hands in an I-don't-know-what-to-say spread. "I still can't believe you worked through all of this in your free time. And I can tell by the way you talk that you're as passionate about this business as I am." He took a breath and looked at the kids. "It's nice to have someone who understands and can help me work through this stuff. Marianne is as committed to the business as I am, but she's the business wiz. She doesn't understand the physical details of the job."

He seemed so genuinely touched by her simple act, and amazed she would take the time to do something like this, she had to wonder if random acts of kindness didn't happen much in his life. It seemed odd, given how kind and giving he was, but his gratitude and wonder was obvious.

She'd enjoyed the work—which hadn't felt like work at all, more like the joy and satisfaction that came from working a jigsaw puzzle—and was glad she'd taken the time to do it. Happiness at doing something she loved, while helping him work through a troubling situation, filled her soul and made her feel as light as a helium balloon.

"I'm happy to help, anytime. All you have to do is call."

His eyebrows lifted playfully. "I like the sound of that." He reached across the table and took her hand in his. "Seriously, will you come to the office Tuesday morning and talk to Marianne?"

Sam didn't know what else Marianne would need. Kevin had all the information before him to make a decision and move forward. But if it would make him happy, she'd go.

"Sure. Any particular time?"

His grin turned mischievous. "After I feed you breakfast."

A faucet turned on in her mouth and she had to swallow a couple of times so she didn't drown in her own drool. Her gaze dropped to his swimming trunks, then took a leisurely stroll up the center of his abs to his chest to his chin and settled on his mouth.

"Yum."

Chapter Fifteen

Kevin gathered Sam's hand in his as he listened to the kids giggle and play in the backseat. He was reminded of riding with Marianne in their parents' car, watching Papà hold Mamma's hand as he smiled across the seat at her... much the way Kevin felt compelled to do with Sam.

Even as a child, when he didn't have a clue what relationships were all about, he recognized the significance of that smile and the love flowing between them as their eyes met and held each other captive. He'd been blessed to grow up in a close-knit family with terrific parental role models who taught him *famiglia* always comes first—that no matter what, you take care of your own.

Back then, he wanted a relationship like his parents shared. But the beauty and innocence of childhood segued into young adulthood, complete with a wild, often reckless bachelor lifestyle that left no room for marriage and family.

Fortunately, the Wildman matured and started to think he might want something more significant than work, endless parties, and a revolving door of one-night stands. The idea continued to blossom and take shape within him, until the day Kat arrived on the scene. That day, the idea erupted through the surface and became a living, breathing, constant force.

He watched her and Erik wrestle their way through hell, more than once. But rather than being ripped apart, they grew even closer because of their challenges. They served as each other's rock, crutch, or glass of bubbly. Whatever the situation demanded, the other was there to fulfill the necessary role.

The real megaphone blast that drove the message home loud and clear, in a way he couldn't miss or forget, was the announcement Kat was expecting. His friends' shared joy at creating a life erased all lingering doubts from his mind. He no longer wondered. He *knew* he was missing out on something precious.

As he glanced in the rearview mirror at the kids, a tight fist squeezed his heart, then twisted a few times, making sure he got the point. This… riding in his truck right now… was the future he wanted so badly it sometimes hurt. A mini-me and a mini-her, playing in the back like he and Marianne, while he and his wife traveled life's highways side-by-side.

"Thanks," he said, glancing at Sam from the corner of his eye as he squeezed her hand.

She lifted her head from the headrest, opened her eyes, and gave him a soft, sweet smile that registered as the final you-better-not-fuck-this-up twist to his thumper. "For what?"

"For a great day. I can't remember the last time I had this much fun."

Hadn't he thought the same thing yesterday? Did this mean every day with Sam and Michaela would be better than the last?

"You're forgetting you're the one who provided the pool, drinks, chips… pizza for dinner."

He kissed her palm. "Yeah, but you provided the entertainment."

Her eyebrow shot up and her chin dropped. "I don't remember dancing on the tables or singing karaoke."

"See…" He checked the mirrors and merged into traffic on 501, headed toward Conway. "You and Michaela make me laugh. Being with you makes me happy." He glanced at the kids in his mirror. "Like I said yesterday, I'm sorry about your ankle, but I'm so glad Spencer and I got to spend the weekend with you guys."

"Me too." She glanced over her shoulder and laughed at something Spencer said to Michaela. "She's had a great time… *We've* had a great time." Her gaze skimmed over his torso before landing on his crotch. She bit down on her lip and lifted her heavy-lidded gaze. "It's all been good, but some parts have been unforgettable."

His chest puffed up with pride at having made *his girls'* weekend special. It wasn't over yet, though. He still had plans for a few of those toys he hadn't gotten to last night. Bouncing the sexy vibe back, he said, "There's still more in store for you."

Her mouth formed an "oh" as interest darkened her eyes and shortened her breath. She glanced at the clock and smiled. "Bedtime for Michaela comes early on school nights."

He grinned and stroked her palm before linking their fingers together. Leaning toward her, he said, "It comes early for her mamma, too."

She swallowed hard and nodded, then shifted in her seat, apparently unsure of the best response.

After allowing her to run the possibilities through her mind for a few minutes, he said, "Thanks, again, for helping me with the Vanguard project and for brainstorming with me on the Bellamy job, too. I've been trying to figure out how to get around the drainage field for weeks, but kept getting tripped up by the retention pond. I used to be able to run things by Papà, but he's been in Italy for almost a month, and I don't have anyone else I can trust."

On Friday, all lingering doubts about his future with Lizbeth had vanished. However, had he still questioned whether they might, under miraculous circumstances, be able to work things out, they would've been eviscerated this weekend.

Not only was Sam willing to listen to him, she listened with interest and replied with enthusiasm. She got it. She got him. She understood the job and shared his passion for building something from nothing. Smart as hell, she possessed a tremendous understanding of the business and offered useful feedback on everything he threw at her. He'd already considered some of her suggestions; others were brilliant ideas he never would've come up with on his own.

He didn't know what the future held for him and Sam, but he needed someone who would care enough to listen when he talked. Their understanding of the intricacies of his job wasn't as important as their willingness to allow him to share this part of his life.

"Was your husband a builder, too?"

The left-field question caught her flat-footed and she jerked in response. "Uh… no. He's a lawyer." Based on her tone and the way her lip curled, she believed lawyers were equal to vermin… or maybe a step below. "He didn't understand anything about my job, nor did he care." Her jaw set defiantly and her spine stiffened. "He didn't like his wife being a construction worker to begin with, so when Daddy died and my brothers wanted to sell, he was only too happy to jump in and help." She made quotation marks again, as she had earlier when she used the word *help.*

Jesus, not one person had supported her. Having grown up in a family-first environment, he couldn't imagine how wounded she must be from the betrayal. "How long were you married?"

"Five years." She glanced into the back and lowered her voice. "Well, legally five years. I have no idea how long he was faithfully married… you know, before he moved on but forgot to tell me."

Kevin stiffened and his heart kerthunked erratically. "You mean he had an affair?"

"According to him, our marriage had been over for a while. I was just too stupid to realize it, and he failed to tell me. At least until I caught him with his secretary bent over his desk."

Kevin's breath caught in his throat as Sam's words floated out and settled over the situation with him and Lizbeth as easily as when she laid the tracing paper over the site plan. If Lizbeth were to find him with Sam right now, he'd be saying the exact same thing.

Their relationship was over and had been for a while. But, like Sam's ex, he hadn't had a conversation with Lizbeth about it. While he hadn't planned on meeting Sam, he did. And he most definitely moved on with someone else, while Lizbeth remained clueless.

Dammit, it wasn't that black and white, though. There were shades of gray with variances of shadows, as well as pockets of light.

Even though neither Lizbeth nor Sam realized he was as big a scumbag as Sam's ex... Okay, wait, he wasn't quite that bad, because he and Lizbeth weren't married. They'd never even discussed marriage, and they didn't have kids...

Shit, am I really debating degrees of scumbagness?

He blew out a breath and squared up in the seat, preparing to defend his position. "Sometimes," he said, going slow, carefully choosing his words, "it's not always black and white. Sometimes things happen, even when we don't set out to hurt those we care about."

She jerked her hand from his as her eyes flashed with fury. "Are you defending him? Are you telling me what he did was okay?"

"No, that's not what I'm saying." Fuck, so much for carefully choosing his words. While trying to defend his own—thus far unknown—actions, he made a major tactical error. He reached for her hand again, but she snatched it out of reach. "I'm sorry, Sam. That was stupid and insensitive and didn't come out the way I intended." He should probably stop now, before he further sunk his ship, but that mother-fucking filter misfired again. "All I meant was I'm sure he didn't mean to hurt you."

Her expression indicated he'd fallen into a bottomless pit of idiocy. "How could it possibly have gone any other way?"

He flipped on his turn signal and pulled into Marianne's neighborhood, grateful for the forced stop to this conversation. "I didn't mean to upset you. Believe me; that's the last thing I want."

One thing this conversation accomplished was to make Sam's position crystal clear. No matter what explanation he gave, she would never understand why he got involved with her before ending his relationship with Lizbeth. And he couldn't blame her. The only thing he could do at this point was hightail his ass to Riverside first thing in the morning and pray Sam never found out.

After the slightly contentious conversation in the car, when Kevin had the audacity to imply Michael's actions were somehow justified, the ride from Marianne's to Sam's was quiet. She had the distinct impression Kevin didn't want to say anything else for fear of getting himself into an even deeper hole… a real possibility given her sour mood.

As he held open the front door and helped her into the house, Sam thought about the paddle and strap in the bottom drawer. *Wonder if he would be interested in role-playing. Him as the bad boy, me as the disciplinarian.* She glanced at him from the corner of her eye and chunked the idea like a hot coal. He'd never go for that and would probably paddle her for having the thought.

He followed her movements as she hop-limped to the fridge for a bottle of water. "Are you sure you don't want me to take you to the doctor first thing in the morning?"

She was getting around much better, but he was still concerned about her managing by herself on Monday. She agreed to let him drive her to work so she didn't need to mess with the clutch. Then she would drive her work car, which was automatic, the rest of the day. The difficulty of maneuvering jobsites, however, still bothered him.

"I'll be fine by morning." She waved her hand dismissively. "Look how much better I am." To prove her point she settled additional weight on her leg, only to snatch her foot up and hiss at the searing pain. She cut her eyes to him and grimaced. "If you don't mind giving me a ride to work, I'll figure it out from there."

"I don't mind at all. I wish I didn't have to go to Riverside." Shadows crossed his eyes and his jaw tensed. "Actually, I want to get this taken care of, but I'd like to be here to help."

"What would you do, drive me to all my jobs and carry me around the sites?"

"Yep." He pulled a grape from the bunch sitting in the strainer on the counter and popped it into his mouth. "I'd be like a dog pissing on a hydrant, marking you as mine, making sure no one else offered to sweep you off your feet."

She laughed while trying to ignore the mushy feelings swirling in her stomach. She liked what he said, even though red lights flashed in warning.

Michaela, who'd been in the back of the house putting up her towel and bathing suit, bolted into the kitchen and took a flying leap at Kevin.

Sam's heart stopped and she lurched forward as Michy's feet left the ground, even though there wasn't a damn thing she could do.

But she didn't need to worry, because even though he wasn't prepared, as soon as he read Michy's intentions, he readied himself and caught her as easily as if the whole thing had been staged… just as Michy expected and trusted.

Sam exhaled in relief and sank against the counter as Michy, oblivious to her mom's reaction, said to Kevin, "Will you read me a book after I finish my bath?"

Kevin snuggled her close. "Sure." His smile was as bright as she'd ever seen and his eyes filled with delight. "What's your favorite?"

"*The Poky Little Puppy.*"

Okay, check that. Now his face was as bright and animated as she'd ever seen. "Me too. When I was little, I always made sure I got home in time for dinner so I didn't have to go to bed hungry."

The mutual love and affection flowing between them shot a wave of panic through Sam.

No, no, no, no, no. Her heart hammered and her palm slid on the Formica countertop at the thought of Michy getting attached to him, only to have him leave in a few weeks—or sooner—when he got bored with them. The only thing a girl could expect from someone called Wildman was heartbreak.

Sam was a big girl and accepted the risk of spending time with Kevin. But she refused to allow her innocent daughter to get caught in her adult games.

She cleared her throat and interrupted the tender moment. "I'll read you a book, sweetie. Kevin probably needs to get going. I'm sure he had things to do this weekend, and we've already taken up enough of his time."

Michaela's face crumpled and she turned sad eyes toward Kevin. Cupping his face in her tiny hands, she said, "You're not staying?"

That, right there, was the reason Sam had to put distance between them. Kevin was so charming and charismatic that in just a few days her daughter had fallen for him.

Oh right, like you haven't?

Yeah, yeah, if she turned the microscope inward, she'd find Michy wasn't the only one who fell hard and fast. But the difference was Sam made a choice to get involved with Kevin and therefore shouldered the risk for getting hurt. Michy was an innocent, doing as children do, following her heart and trusting the adults around her to keep her safe. Just as she had when she made that leap into Kevin's arms.

Sensing a problem, but unable to get a bead on her objection, Kevin's dark eyes fixed on Sam. He stared, as if looking long enough would unlock a great mystery hidden behind her eyes.

His close scrutiny made her feel like shit, but she wouldn't be swayed, so she crossed her arms over her stomach and looked away. Michy was her daughter and if she wanted to read the bedtime story, rather than turning the privilege over to someone else, that was her prerogative. Dammit.

Kevin sat Michy on the counter and tucked a blond curl behind her ear. "I think your mamma wants to read your book tonight. I'll do it another time. Okay?" Michy nodded and tried to keep looking at him, but dropped her gaze to the floor. "But you're not staying?"

"No, *piccolina,* not tonight."

Michy's gaze snapped up. "What's *piccolina?* I thought I was a foll… a foll…"

Kevin grinned. "A *folletta* is a pixie. *Piccolina* means little one."

The moment of disappointment over, she grinned and clapped her hands. "Will you teach me Italian?"

"Noooo…" He laughed and kissed her on the cheek. "If I did that, I'd have to learn a third language, so you won't know when I'm saying bad words." He looked at the jar on the counter filled with coins and a few dollar bills. "I'd be broke in a week."

"Okay, let Kevin put you down so you can get your bath and get in bed. I'll check on you in a minute."

Kevin picked her up to set her on her feet, but Michy wrapped her arms around his neck and held on tight. "Thank you for taking me and Mommy swimming yesterday and today."

Kevin's eyes drifted shut and his breath left in a whoosh as he returned the hug with what appeared to be a bone-crushing grip. "You're welcome. We'll do it again soon."

The mutual affection expressed in their faces tightened Sam's throat. She didn't want Michy to be hurt, but she also couldn't help but wonder if he wore a similar expression while holding her.

Jesus, Sam, don't be stupid. He's a fling. A bed companion. A sex toy. Nothing more. Remember that.

As Michy disappeared down the hall and into the bathroom, Kevin cleared his throat and turned on Sam. "You obviously didn't want me reading to her, but I don't know why."

"She's getting too attached and that's not good."

He cocked his head and thought for a minute. "All right, I'll admit I'm getting kind of attached to her"—his eyes darkened and he smiled softly—"and her mamma. But I don't see the problem."

An internal battle waged within Sam. She'd like to look at the surface and believe everything would be fine. He'd shown her nothing but kindness since the moment they met up on the beach. Even at his job site, he'd responded the way anyone in his situation would, but he wasn't rude or disrespectful. He was one of the few men in the industry who didn't treat her poorly just because she was a woman.

Today at the pool, he shared a lot of himself with her. He talked about his jobs and asked her opinion, and he listened intently when she gave it. He'd been interested in her point of view and excited about an option she'd thrown out for handling a particular drainage problem.

She couldn't ask for anyone to be kinder to Michaela. And seeing the close bond he had with Spencer, hearing about the things they did together, proved he wasn't only capable of caring for kids, but he genuinely loved them.

Then there was the sex. Just thinking about it made her temperature rise. She definitely wanted more and couldn't wait to see how he planned to carry out the fantasy threesome.

But she couldn't allow Michy to get hurt while she acted out a few sexual games.

Resolve in place, she said, "Men leave; hearts get broken. I understand that's the way life works. But she's a child and it's my job to protect her from as much pain and disappointment as possible. So far, I've failed miserably. I was blindsided by my dad's death and Michael's leaving. But this I can control, and I won't allow her to get more attached, only to end up hurt."

His head tilted awkwardly and his brow dropped into a severe frown as his eyes darkened dangerously. "How can you possibly compare me to either of those situations? I haven't done…" His voice trailed off and he rubbed his hand across the back of his neck while chomping on the inside of his cheek.

She was again reminded of a lion stalking the jungle, looking for prey as he prowled around her small kitchen. Anger rolled off him in waves before he took a handful of deep breaths and calmed slightly. Stopping with his hands on his hips, he pegged her with a fierce stare. "Do you honestly think your dad, had he been given a choice, would've left you?"

"Of course not, but that doesn't change the fact that he did. He not only physically left me, but he left me in a terrible bind with my family. I had no way out." Even though she sounded childish and knew the argument was absurd, she couldn't help the returning sense of loss and feelings of abandonment filling her chest, drowning her in sorrow all over again.

And then there was Michael. He did have a choice, but he hadn't cared enough to handle things differently.

She'd do anything to never feel that way again and would move Heaven and Earth to prevent Michy from experiencing an ounce of that pain.

Kevin stopped in front of her and took her chin in his fingers, holding her face steady, forcing her to meet his stare. "I'm not your dad or your brothers or your ex." His eyes flashed and he winced as the muscle in his jaw worked. "I don't know where this thing with us is going, but I want it to go somewhere. I care about you, and I adore that little girl. Please, Sam, give me a chance."

Chapter Sixteen

$\mathcal{L}$eaning back in a lawn chair, feet kicked up on the railing of his deck overlooking the Pamlico River, Kevin glared at the mosquito circling his ankle, trying to decide on the prime spot to stop and dine. He watched and waited, and when the little fucker landed, Kevin smacked it into oblivion. After his long, grueling day of accomplishing nothing, it felt good to beat the shit out of something… even if it was his own leg.

"Wow, a blow like that would take down a jumbo jet."

Startled by Kat's voice, he jerked in her direction off to the side of the deck, which threw his precariously balanced chair off-kilter. With arms flailing like he was in the fight of his life, he got the front legs planted on the ground and the chair stabilized. He glanced at the beer foaming over on his hand and cursed. "Damn, I nearly lost it." *And not just the beer.* He stood and headed in her direction. "What are you doing here, *piccola?*"

Once upon a time, Erik would've ripped Kevin's heart out for calling Kat baby, but they were well beyond that now, and all of them could laugh at the now-fond memory of Erik nearly splitting him wide open over Kat.

"I came to ask you the same thing," she said, crossing the deck to meet him. "Erik's at the Coastal Preservation board meeting—"

"Shit, I forgot." Since he hadn't planned on being in Riverside today, he hadn't given the meeting any thought. He checked his watch, only to find it was six-thirty and the meeting had started at six.

"I wondered why your garage door was open, so I came over to check on you."

"Thanks, *piccola*." He kissed her on the cheek, then put his hand to the small of her back to lead her toward the door. "You want to go inside?"

She took a deep breath and gazed out at the river. "No, I'm wearing bug spray. I'm good out here."

He grabbed another chair from the corner of the deck and held it steady while she got settled. *"Come sta il bambino?"*

"Dammit, you're going to teach this baby Italian, aren't you?" She tried to look annoyed, but couldn't hold the narrowed eyes, and her lips twitched rather than turned down. "I'll forever be wondering what you two are saying."

"I promise not to teach him the bad words."

She snorted. "Yeah, right." A wide smile split her face as she absently rubbed the baby bump… which was more like a mountain. "Doctor says he-she-it probably weighs around five pounds and everything seems to be on track."

Since they weren't finding out the baby's sex until birth day, Erik came up with the ridiculous nickname so they had something to call the *bambino,* other than "baby." Kat spent the better part of six months arguing against the name, but apparently, she'd given up the fight. Seeing the joy on her face and sharing this moment with her was the brightest spot in his godforsaken, show-me-a-bridge-I-can-jump-off-of day.

"That's fantastic. I can't wait to be an uncle again."

"And a godfather."

"Yeah." His heart swelled with love for the unborn child… then cracked a little as he thought about the baby girl he'd held last night, but had to let go. At least Sam hadn't completely shut him out.

She agreed to keep seeing him, with the understanding he wouldn't arrive until after Michy was in bed. God, the rule chapped his ass, but he understood her reasons and would do whatever he needed to prove he was in for the long haul… or as long as she let him stay.

Shaking off the creeping melancholy, he said, "At the party the other night, there were a ton of jokes about me looking like a mob hit man. Wait until everyone finds out I really am a godfather."

She laughed at his Al Capone impersonation, but her smile faded as she glanced to the decking and the six-pack next to his chair.

"I've only had two," he said, holding up the carton for her to see. "I know you and Erik are worried…" He released a slow, deep breath. "You had reason to be, but I've been working on it this weekend. I only had one on Saturday and none yesterday. I promise, it's all good and under control."

She wanted to believe him, but her eyes dropped to the bottle in his hand. "Then why are you sitting here, drinking alone? Has something happened between you and Lizbeth?"

"No," he growled. "Nothing's happened with Lizbeth, which is the problem."

Kat eased back in her chair and twisted at an odd angle, making room for he-she-it under her ribcage. "I'm not following."

He sipped his beer while debating how much to say. He hated involving Kat in his bullshit, but she might have an idea where Lizbeth had run off to… And running was exactly what she'd done.

When he couldn't reach her by cell early this morning, he suspected something was amiss. When he spoke with her assistant and found out she'd gone to Raleigh for the day and couldn't be reached, he knew she'd gone into hiding. She never left without telling him where she'd be, or without making sure she left a detailed itinerary of how to reach her every moment of the day.

Except today, of course, when he'd specifically told her to expect him.

"You don't happen to know where Lizbeth is, do you?"

"No, I haven't talked to her since the party." Disbelief clouded her eyes. "You don't know where she is?"

He threw his hand in the air and gave a dry laugh. "Hard to believe, huh?"

"Erik was pretty upset after the party on Friday about something she'd done, but he wouldn't go into details." She glanced to his beer again. "What's going on? From the beginning."

He took a big gulp, then dove into his spiel about not being happy, but not wanting to hurt her before the wedding, yada, yada, yada. In the beginning, the logic made sense, but as he sat here recounting his sob story to Kat, thinking about Sam and all he had to lose, the whole thing sounded asinine. By the time he finished, he was more furious with himself than ever.

Kat quietly listened, allowing him to ramble until he ran out words. After a long silence, during which no one spoke but the crickets and a bullfrog, she said, "But?"

"But what?"

She huffed at his stupidity. "Something's changed and you're ready to end things now."

Her steady gaze made him squirm in the chair like Spencer did when he did something wrong and was in hot water. Kevin wasn't ending the relationship with Lizbeth because of Sam. That decision had been made before they met. The increased urgency, however, had everything to do with Sam, and that created a fair amount of guilt along with a touch of shame. Rather than respond verbally, he nodded, then looked away.

"You're trying my patience here. What's changed?"

Her response sounded like something Sam would say, and, despite the seriousness of their conversation, he laughed. "Sorry," he said. "You reminded me of someone."

When she failed to see the humor, he sighed and ran his thumb and forefinger across his forehead. "I've sort of met someone."

"Oh, this is good." The laugh in Kat's voice brought his attention back to her. "Does Erik know? Does he get a chance at payback?"

He laughed, remembering the night he and the guys taught Kat to play cards. Only, they hadn't taught her *all* the rules, thereby ensuring she lost pretty much every hand. The more they laughed and joked and poured shots down her, the more pissed off Erik became.

Things continued to deteriorate the next morning when Kevin offered to take Kat home, knowing how badly it would rip Erik to shreds. He'd made the comment to force Erik to get his head out of his ass and see what a good thing he had with Kat, but it had taken Erik a long time to forgive him.

"No, he doesn't know."

Her grin grew to obscene proportions. "Karma is a cruel mistress." She sobered. "So you've met someone, and you don't want to wait until after the wedding to make a move."

"Yeah, uhh…" He tugged at his ear and stared at the water. "That line's kinda already been crossed."

"Oh." There wasn't any censure in her voice, only quiet under-standing. "What's her name?"

"Sam." At her quirked eyebrow, he said, "Samantha is her given name. I wouldn't recommend using it."

"Does she know about Lizbeth?"

"Hell no." He shook his head as panic clogged his airway.

Kat quietly contemplated the situation and, after several uncomfortable minutes, said, "You're one of the most honest and upfront men I've ever met. I understand why you didn't want to break up with Lizbeth until after the wedding, but…" She scooted around in the chair so she could see him face to face. "Why did you move into this new situation so soon?"

"It just happened." He ran a hand over his face at the lame excuse. "She's a building inspector and we met through work." He grinned, thinking of their initial meeting. "The first time we met, she shut my ass down. Well, not *my* ass. The job. Had she shut my ass down, I wouldn't be in this predicament."

His chest filled with warmth at Sam's willingness to go above and beyond her responsibilities to help him. "While I was here Friday evening," he said, "she was at home, working on one of my projects, finding a solution to my problem."

"She certainly sounds more like your type."

"She is. She grew up around construction and loves it. She always wanted to go to work with her dad, but he wouldn't let her until she was big enough to climb into the truck by herself. She's a tiny thing, barely over five feet now. I can only imagine how little she was then…" As his mouth ran away at one hundred mph, an image of Michaela flashed into his mind. "Actually, I have a perfect picture of what she would've looked like. Her name is Michaela, and she's the sweetest little girl in the world."

He paused and swallowed the knot in his throat. He'd fallen so hard for that little girl he couldn't stand the thought of not ever seeing her again. And that was nothing compared to the way he felt about her mamma. How in the hell had this happened in such a short time?

"Michaela is her daughter?"

As Kat absently ran circles over her belly, he wondered what Sam looked like pregnant? How had labor and delivery been for her? As ridiculous as it was, he found himself growing incredibly sad because he'd missed the miracle of Michaela's birth.

"Yeah. She has curly blond hair and big blue eyes. She's cute as can be and precocious as Spencer. The two of them together are a mess." He couldn't hide the silly grin breaking loose. "This past weekend with them was the best I've ever had."

He shook his head and sobered. "But if Sam ever found out I was involved with someone when we got together, she'd never get over it, nor would she forgive me."

Kat frowned. "That doesn't sound like a very forgiving or understanding partner."

"She has serious trust issues, and for good reason. Everyone in her life has let her down in one way or another. Her dad didn't take care of the business side of things, so when he died suddenly, she was at the mercy of her mom and brothers. Her brothers doubted her ability to carry on the family business, and her mother sided with them. They sold the business out from under her, leaving her with nothing. Shortly after, her husband decided their marriage wasn't working and found someone else—his secretary."

Kat sucked in air between her teeth and grimaced. "Ouch. I can see how that would make it difficult to trust again, but still…" She winced. "You're gonna screw up from time to time, just like Erik. Just like me." She grinned and batted her eyes while scrunching up her shoulders. "I know you think I'm perfect, but I'm really not." She grew serious and bit her upper lip. "If she doesn't have the capacity to forgive and move on, your life will be very difficult."

"I don't know about all that, Kat, or if the relationship will last forever. I do know I can't be tacked onto the long line of people who failed her. I just can't."

Kat nodded and took a deep breath. "So what are you going to do?"

He turned sad puppy dog eyes on her. "You wanna help a poor, worthless son of a bitch out?"

She eyed him suspiciously. "How?"

"Lizbeth isn't answering my calls or returning any of my messages."

She groaned. "Shit, you want me to call her." It wasn't a question or a no, but she wasn't happy about being dragged into his stupid high school-ish drama.

"No, I just want to use your phone. She might pick up if she thinks you're calling. I don't want to cause you any problems, but I need help. Hell, I'll throw my phone in the river, say it went overboard and can't be used and that's why I'm calling from your number."

Kat sighed, and with her belly leading the way, pushed to her feet. "You don't have to go that far. I have a working relationship with Lizbeth that I'd like to preserve for the shelter's sake, but you're family. I'll do whatever's needed to help you make this right. Come on over to the house."

Kevin grabbed Kat and squeezed her tight, which wasn't all that much considering a watermelon lay between them. "Thank you. I know this is childish, stupid bullshit. And I didn't want to do this over the phone, but she's not giving me any choice."

As they crossed toward the steps, she said, "I just hope Lizbeth doesn't make your life hell over the next few weeks."

"You and me both." However, knowing Lizbeth, and based on the way she handled things today, that would require a miracle.

After three unsuccessful calls to Lizbeth, Kevin was done. Beyond done. He'd tried calling from Kat's cell and their house phone with no luck. His only option was to leave a message. He couldn't think of a shittier way to end a long-term relationship, but Lizbeth hadn't given him any choice. He refused to go back to Myrtle Beach with this hanging over his head.

The third time her voicemail picked up, he left a short, to-the-point message.

"Lizbeth, since you disappeared and refuse to take my calls, I'm assuming you know why I came to Riverside. Not being available doesn't change the ending. Call me when you find time and we'll work out the details of how to handle things over the next few weeks."

He hung up and turned to Kat. "Too harsh?"

"I don't think so," she said with a slow, sad shake of her head and helpless lift of her shoulder. "You told her you were coming to Riverside to talk, right?"

"Yeah." He thought back to his explosion the previous day. "She was whining about the caterer and a potential storm…" He blew out a breath and rolled his neck in a circle. "I went off on her. She wanted me to tell her everything would be okay, and I couldn't. I told her we needed to talk and haven't heard from her since."

"I'd say you're right. She thought by avoiding you she'd prevent the inevitable." She crossed the kitchen and wrapped him in a supportive hug. "You did your best to talk to her face to face, but she's not cooperating." She let go and stepped back. "You and Lizbeth never made sense to me, but I thought my own prejudice clouded my judgment. Even though that's not how you wanted to do things, since you made that call, your shoulders aren't hunched, your brow isn't furrowed." She scrunched her nose up and grinned awkwardly. "You don't look like a bomb with two seconds left on the clock."

He wrapped his arm around her neck and kissed the top of her head. "Thanks." He felt guilty for leaving a cold message on Lizbeth's voicemail, but Kat was right. Who would've thought guilt was lighter than the emotional baggage he'd been carrying around for the past six months? "Mind if I take one for the road?" he asked, grabbing a bottle of water from their refrigerator.

"Of course not. Help yourself to anything you like. Do you want me to fix you something to eat?"

"Naw, I'm good." He gave a naughty smile. "I have plans tonight, so I need to get going."

"Oh, boy." She put her hands over her ears. "La-la-la-la-la. I don't even want to know."

"No, ma'am," he said with a grin. "You don't." Halfway to the door, he stopped and pivoted around. "Hey, do you have an unwashed shirt of Erik's that smells like him?"

Kat's mouth fell open and she blinked a half dozen times before regaining her composure. Resting her arms on top of her belly, she cocked her hip to the side and said, "I always knew there was a massive bromance between you two, simmering just below the surface. I never thought you'd go so far as to ask for one of his shirts to sleep with, though."

"Damn, I thought we'd kept it well hidden all these years." Heading toward their master bedroom, he said, "Can I have a little bottle of his cologne, too?"

Kat stood flat-footed, mouth dropped open. "You're serious? You want one of his shirts? And his cologne? What are you up to?"

Kevin laughed at the thought of her finding out his plans for Erik's shirt. Erik would want details. Kat would be la-la-la-laing again. Continuing toward their bedroom suite, he said, "Again, you don't want to know."

Chapter Seventeen

*H*e hadn't figured out all the details of making Sam's fantasy three-some a reality, but he knew who to call to put the pieces together. Lucas Steele, owner of Myrtle Beach's premier kink club, had seen and probably done everything possible. A master of mind games, at least in the sexual sense, if anyone could help Kevin pull this off, it was Lucas.

Once he got into an area with consistent cell phone coverage, he called Lucas's club. When the front desk hostess answered, he asked for Lucas, not *Master* Lucas, as protocol dictated.

Right on cue, the sweet, soft-spoken sub said, "You mean, Master Lucas?"

Within the scene and especially at the club, everyone referred to Lucas as Master—something Kevin refused to do, mostly just to irritate his friend. Kevin understood why those within the lifestyle showed Lucas the respect he'd clearly earned and deserved. But he wasn't in the lifestyle, and unless at the club or within a setting requiring the respect, he refused to call his friend Master.

It had become a thorn of sorts he enjoyed pricking Lucas with when the opportunity presented itself. Like now. "That's what I said… Lucas. Tell him that's who I asked for too, no Master." He chuckled at her small gasp.

"Yes, sir," she squeaked. He really shouldn't mess with Lucas's subs like this. The poor thing was probably terrified Lucas would take a pound of flesh from her for addressing him so disrespectfully, regardless of Kevin's command. But Lucas would never punish the messenger, and Kevin couldn't pass up the opportunity to aggravate.

Twenty minutes later, Lucas picked up. "Mazze, been a long time. To what do I owe this pleasure?"

"Man, I didn't even tell her my name. You're good. Tell me something. If I'd asked for *Master* Lucas, would you've answered faster?"

Lucas's deep, rumbling laughter rolled across the line. "Maybe. Poor Chrissie is going to need a ton of aftercare because of you. I thought she would break down trying to deliver your message." The sound of the club dissipated and Kevin figured Lucas had gone into his private office. "What's up?"

"I need help—"

"Oh, really?" Lucas interrupted, his amusement clear. "You should've thought of that before you traumatized my sub."

Unconcerned, Kevin continued. "My girl wants to play out a fantasy threesome, with only the two of us. Something I'm happy to do if I can figure out the logistics of making it real. I know…" Kevin exhaled in defeat. "Okay, I'll concede this point. You're a master of the mindfuck, so how do I get my girl to believe there's two of us when it's just me?"

"Hang on. I need to write this down… Mazze conceded…"—Kevin could make out the sound of a pencil scribbling on a piece of paper—"and referred to me as Master… What's the date?"

"Yeah, yeah, yeah…" Kevin laughed. "Don't get used to it; it won't happen again."

"We'll see."

"Can I make this work or what?"

"Yeah, absolutely. This'll be fun. Here's what we're going to do—"

"We?"

"Yeah, we."

Lucas laid out the plan while Kevin drove. Thirty minutes outside of Myrtle Beach, he called Sam. He hadn't talked to her all day, other than a brief text to check on her ankle, and he was surprised at the tremble in his fingers as he dialed her number.

There were several possible reasons for the geyser of sweat on his neck and lip: fear she'd somehow found out what he'd been doing; concern his planned threesome would fail miserably; or a subconscious worry she'd changed her mind about continuing to see him, even on a limited basis.

Whatever the reason, bats were bouncing off the cavernous walls of his gut, making him twitchy as hell. "Jesus, you'd think I was seventeen—"

"Hey." The sound of her happy voice erased all concerns, past, present, and future, and put a smile on his face.

After twenty minutes of general conversation, he got down to business. "Michy's in bed, right?"

"At eleven o'clock? Of course."

"Good, because you're about to have company."

Pause. "I am?" She tried to sound cool and aloof, but he caught the hitch in her voice.

He trusted Lucas's instincts with this type of thing, but as he ran over the plan in his mind one last time, his heart hammered erratically and he struggled with a little hitch of his own. "Go to the bedroom. I'm about to give you a shopping list."

"What if I don't want to?"

He grinned at her attempt to be distant, even through her heavy breathing.

"Oh, you want to. Now, get the blindfold, those cuffs buried in the bottom left corner of the drawer... the soft ones. I don't want to hurt your wrists. The medium butt plug, lube, a towel, condoms."

Her strangled breath gave him pause, until he realized it didn't come from fear, but rather from her struggling to get down the hallway with her hurt foot. When the bedroom door clicked shut, he continued.

"I want you on the bed on your hands and knees, naked, blindfolded, medium plug inserted, your wrists cuffed together."

The bottom drawer slid open. "I don't normally do well with orders, but you're pretty hot, so in your case I'll make an exception."

Staying in Dom mode—as Lucas called it—to get her in the right frame of mind, he stifled a laugh and kept his voice low and commanding. "You'll be well rewarded for your obedience."

Shit, he should've thought about the lock on the door before she got all the way back to the bedroom. "Is there a key hidden outside, or do you need to go back and unlock the door? It won't be unlocked long. We'll be there in about seven minutes."

Forget the hitch. A full-on gasp burst through the line this time. "Kevin—"

"Sam." He made his voice snap like a whip. "Don't overthink this. I asked you the other day if you trusted me, and you said yes. Do you or not?"

Her brief hesitation concerned him, but her voice was strong and sure when she spoke. "Yes. Yes, I do. The key is under the terracotta frog at the bottom of the steps."

He pulled the phone away from his ear and looked at the screen like that would change the words she'd spoken. *The terracotta frog at the bottom of the stairs?* Could she be more obvious? He sighed and shook his head and made a mental note to get her something more secure than a freaking terracotta frog.

Refocusing on the here and now, he said, "You're down to five minutes. We'll see you soon."

With shaking fingers and a pounding heart, Sam did as Kevin asked… correction… told her. Her head spun and her breath came in such short, shallow gasps she feared she might pass out. But that would ruin everything, and she wasn't going to miss this chance to live out her fantasy. She didn't understand the "we," but she said she trusted him. She needed to step up and prove it.

Five minutes wasn't a lot of time, so she worked quickly and efficiently. She tossed her T-shirt onto the chair in the corner, her bra, pants, and panties followed. She hobbled to the bathroom, grabbed a towel, and spread it out in the middle of the bed. Next stop, the toy drawer.

A rush of adrenaline shot through her as she dug to the bottom and found the fuzzy cuffs she'd never worn, then gathered the plug, lube, and condoms. Her hands shook so badly with nervous energy, she needed four tries to get the lid twisted off the damn lube.

"Breathe, Sam, breathe. You have the chance to live out a fantasy. Don't freak yourself out and screw things up. You'll never forgive yourself if you don't follow through with this." She closed her eyes and took a couple of deep breaths while picturing Kevin's full bottom lip and warm, rich eyes.

Dizzy wooziness over, she held the silicone plug in her left hand and squirted a generous portion of lube onto the blunt tip. She laid the open container on the nightstand where it would be accessible to—*deep breath*—them, then used her index finger to coat the entire toy. She climbed onto all fours, took a deep breath to relax her muscles, and pressed the head against her tight opening.

After playing with the Double Dong, the plug wasn't much of a challenge, so within seconds she had it seated in place. Normally, she would take her time with the play and enjoy the sensations zinging through her as the numerous anal nerve endings were stimulated. In this case, the plug was foreplay rather than the main event. The muscles needed to be loosened and prepared for… them?

Sam, what the hell are you doing?

A shiver racked her, forcing her into another pep talk. "Shit. Don't overthink this. Think about Kevin. Enjoy this experience with Kevin. Keep your focus on Kevin." With the plug and her attitude adjusted, she wrapped the blindfold around her head, but left her eyes uncovered while slipping on the cuffs.

Once linked together, she used her thumbs to slide the blindfold into place, shifted her leg so her ankle was comfortable, and rested her forehead on her cuffed wrists, so she didn't topple over with the increased shivering.

To say she was self-conscious about being in the middle of the bed, her hands cuffed, ass sticking up in the air with a protruding plug was a major understatement—hello, this was way worse than being naked on Main Street—but she reminded herself, again, to put her embarrassment aside and trust Kevin.

The task was easy while alone, but the second the front door opened, she broke out in a sheen of sweat, the cool air in the room brushed her slick skin, and she trembled almost uncontrollably.

Voices.

Multiple voices.

Two male voices… two sets of footsteps. *Dear sweet Jesus in heaven above, he really brought a friend.*

Panic battled with the earlier excitement… and won.

The voices stopped as they neared Michaela's room, then picked up again as they reached the end of the hallway and Sam's room. The door squeaked and Kevin said, "Hey, sugar."

She couldn't take it anymore. She had to know who came into the room with him. She pressed her thumbs against the blindfold, but a swift smack across the ass made her jump. Instinctively, she reached back to soothe her stinging butt, forgetting her hands were linked.

She listed to the side and forward, nearly face planting on the bed before Kevin grabbed her shoulders and steadied her. "No cheating. I told you to wear the blindfold for a reason."

Her breathing was so fast and unsteady, she thought she might pass out. She was definitely going to throw up. She turned her head to him and said, "I'm scared. I changed my mind. I can't do this. Untie me."

From the other side of the room, near the dresser, a man with a deep, soothing voice said, "Kevin, touch her. Reassure her." The voice sounded odd, somewhat distorted, but she was so overwhelmed she couldn't sort through the particulars.

Another man—a stranger—stood in her bedroom, while she knelt on hands and knees, blindfolded, handcuffed, and totally helpless. Oh, and she had a plug up her ass. "Kevin," she screamed. "Please help me up."

"Don't be afraid," his friend said as Kevin pressed a kiss to her temple. "Kevin will take good care of you. Do you trust him?"

She swallowed roughly, forcing the nausea to retreat, then went to war against the tear threatening to spring from her eye. The bed dipped and Kevin's scent surrounded her. Drawing the woodsy scent into her lungs like a calming dose of Xanax, she clung to the familiarity and reminded herself he was here… and he'd arranged this for her.

He cupped her face in his hands and she instinctively turned her cheek into his palm. The rough heat sent a soothing current through her system, further settling her. He eased the blindfold up, but with his face right in front of hers, the only thing she saw was his eyes… his dark, warm, beautiful eyes she'd come to love.

"Lucas—"

Lucas cleared his throat roughly, which caused Kevin's eyes to narrow. "*Master* Lucas asked you a question."

She held his gaze and allowed his strength to carry her through the fear. This was Kevin. He'd never let anything bad happen to her. He'd protected and taken care of her and, in this particular moment, he was trying to make a long-time fantasy a reality. All she had to do was have faith.

"Sam, answer the question. Do you trust me?"

"Yes," she whispered, nodding her head as much as she could with him holding her tightly. "I trust you." She took a few deep breaths and pulled herself together. "Thank you."

His eyes softened as his breath slowly leaked out. "You're welcome, *amore mio.*" He pressed his lips to hers in a sweet, tender kiss that quickly turned hot and hungry. "I'm slipping the blindfold back into place. You don't have to do anything but trust us to make you feel good… very, *very* good."

As soon as he stood and moved away, cold air rushed in and surrounded her, allowing fear to grab hold and start dragging her away again.

While she battled her anxiety, Lucas said, "You're a beautiful woman, Samantha." The bed on the other side dipped, and a spicy, unfamiliar scent drifted over her. "If you were mine, I'd make you leave this gorgeous blond hair loose all the time." A hand, firmer and heavier than Kevin's, stroked her head. "So soft and silky."

He gathered her hair in his hand and tugged, while another hand pressed against the front of her chest. "I want you up on your knees—"

"But not all the way back on your heels," Kevin interjected. "We don't want you putting extra pressure on your hurt ankle."

"No," Lucas said. "We don't want that. But we do want access to every part of you, so spread your legs wide."

She gulped and allowed them to move her into position—legs wide, spine straight, linked hands on thighs—while also protecting her ankle from additional weight and strain.

Lucas tugged sideways on her head so her face rotated toward him. Teeth nipped at her lips as a hand palmed her breast. A gentle massage turned rough as he compressed her breast in his hand and pinched her nipple between his finger and thumb, then tugged. "As sweet as your mouth is, I bet this is even better. Kevin, you love these luscious breasts and nipples, don't you?"

"Yeah," Kevin said. "Be grateful for this opportunity. It's the only one you'll get."

Lucas laughed and wrapped his lips around her tight nipple and sucked. He licked and laved, then latched on with his teeth and pulled. Zings of awareness lit up all of her erogenous zones, and she arched her back, giving him greater access, subconsciously begging for more.

"So responsive," Lucas murmured.

The hand in her hair relaxed and slid down her back to the plug. As he tugged on the plug, she battled between leaning forward so he could play with the plug easier, or staying upright in hopes he would continue the wonderful things his mouth was doing to her breasts.

He pulled the plug out, almost completely, then pushed it back in. "Oh, God." Comfortable with Lucas's touch, she shed all self-consciousness and fear. Lost to the moment of being kissed and stroked, she moaned with pleasure and allowed them to take her somewhere she'd never been before. "So good."

They moved the plug out... in... out... in... in a slow, maddening rhythm that set her on fire, and she rocked back and forth, craving still more. No more plug. She wanted them. "Please."

"You are so beautiful... I can't wait to bury my cock in this sweet ass. I do get the ass, right?"

"Do you want me in front or back?" Kevin asked, close to her face on the opposite side of Lucas.

Her brain was humming and buzzing with overstimulation, much like the rest of her body, but his question required no thought. "Front. I want you holding me." She'd gotten used to Lucas's voice, scent, and touch, but Kevin was the anchor she needed in order to keep going forward. "I *need* you holding me."

A low groan filled the room, and one of them swallowed roughly. "You get the ass, Lucas. We'll be right back, sugar."

The bed shifted again, a drawer opened and closed, and Lucas said, "You have quite a collection, Samantha." A paddle smacked skin, and she gasped, spinning her head toward the dresser even though she couldn't see through the blindfold. Lucas laughed, "I understand you have a penchant for spankings. Is that true?"

She gulped and nodded.

"Maybe Kevin will let me play with you at the club sometime. I'd love to see your beautiful ass glowing pink."

"We'll talk about that later," Kevin said before kissing her cheek and jaw. She tilted her head in the opposite direction, exposing her neck while arching her back, encouraging him to keep going. His tongue slipped along her shoulder and down to her breast with a gentler touch than Lucas's.

Lucas's harsher touch had ramped her up, but Kevin's loving and less aggressive touch tugged at her heart. He stroked her back and ass, tugged at the plug, and laved her breast with his mouth and tongue until she was on the verge of a massive orgasm.

But before she blasted off for outer space, he stopped, leaving her trembling and aching for release. "Kevin, please. Enough teasing."

"Are you sure you want to do this?"

He laughed as she nodded furiously. "Yes, dammit, I'm sure. Now."

"I'm gonna remove the plug and get you ready for Lucas."

Her muscles contracted, trying to hold the plug in place, even though she wanted it gone to make room for Lucas. She jumped as a cold stream of lube ran down her butt crack, then shivered as Kevin plucked her clit and stroked her sex with one hand, while the other worked lube into her. "If you were any wetter, we wouldn't need lube."

His hands left her and the bed shifted again, at the end, on one side, the other side, and finally, near her head. "You're going to straddle me, so I can fuck you from the front, while Lucas takes you from the rear. Lucas will go first." Kevin swept her hair over her shoulder and brushed his hand down her neck to her breast. "Then it's my turn." His voice was rough and filled with hungry intent.

She had the impression Kevin was propping up the pillows to recline against. When he was ready, he wrapped his hands around her waist and helped her onto his lap.

The plan to let Lucas go first flew out the window as his erection rubbed her clit and sex, so close, yet so far away. She wiggled around, trying to get them aligned so she could slide onto him.

A hand slapped her ass, getting her attention as intended. "Stop moving." He pulled her down onto his chest, which tilted her butt up… for Lucas. A palm ran down her spine, over her cheek, then into the crease of her ass. "Loop your wrists around my neck."

"Are you ready for me, Samantha?" Lucas asked from the end of the bed.

Her earlier anxiety had evaporated, leaving behind nothing but nervous excitement and anticipation. "Yes." Pleading desperation filled her voice. She'd never been so turned on in her life and she might explode. Not in an oh-God-that-feels-so-good orgasm, but from frustration ripping her apart.

In the next heartbeat, Lucas pressed against her entrance, larger than the medium plug and possibly even larger than the Double Dong.

Her heart pounded and her breathing faltered as she reflexively clenched her muscles against him.

"Whoa, what are you doing?" Kevin asked. "Take a deep breath and relax and let him in."

"This is your fantasy, Samantha. Two men loving you, taking you from the front and back at the same time. Filling you to the point of near bursting. Relax and push back."

Lucas's soft, melodic voice soothed her and compelled her to do as he said. "Is he bigger than you?" she asked Kevin with a gasp as Lucas breached her opening.

"No, sugar. He's not," Kevin said, ruffling the hair at her temple.

A laugh echoed through the room. "You wish."

"Shit, I'll never be able to take all of you"—she panted—"either of you." Trembling started in her fingers, spread to her hands, and rushed up her arms and shoulders before shooting down her spine.

Kevin's arm around her waist tightened and drew her closer. "Feel my chest against your breasts." She diverted her attention away from Lucas and focused on her breasts, smashed against the hard planes of Kevin's chest, a chest hair tickling her just below her neck.

"Feel my thighs spreading you open." She moved her attention down her body. Her stomach muscles clenched and tight against his hard abs... The slight burn in her thighs from being split wide over his hips...

"Feel his cock filling your ass, just like you've always wanted."

She drew in deep breaths as Lucas pressed in a small amount, then withdrew. Slow in. Slow out. Each penetrating thrust breached her muscles farther than the time before, sending heated electrical charges through her nervous system.

Her mind shut down and her body took over. With her arms wrapped around Kevin's neck, she didn't have a lot of mobility, but she rocked back and forth, encouraging Lucas to go deeper. "More."

"Oh yeah," Kevin ground out. "Good girl."

Lucas was huge, and she moaned with pleasure while ignoring the slight discomfort of being stretched farther than ever before.

Kevin's breathing rasped in her ear as she rocked against Lucas. "We're going to put a mirror on your ceiling, so I can watch him fuck you next time." A few more thrusts and Kevin exhaled sharply. "He's all the way in."

"This is so good." She groaned as Lucas stroked in and out, while Kevin massaged her clit and prepared to enter her. Lucas was definitely larger than the Double Dong, as was Kevin, and she feared the two of them entering her at the same time would split her open, but she found herself writhing against him, whispering, "I need you. Please."

Something pressed against her hips and thighs. Then Kevin's hands were around her waist, lifting her over him. With him positioned at the entrance of her sex, she dropped onto him in one swift motion. He moaned and she cried out as the two men filled her to capacity.

Holy God. The Double Dong was intense, but nothing could compare to this. Two men stretching her and filling her until she thought she might burst.

Kevin started off slow and steady, which gave her time to adjust to the unfamiliarity of having two men in her at once. After a few minutes, slow and steady wasn't going to win the race, so she rocked back and forth, urging him to step up the pace.

As always, he obliged her wishes and took her from zero to sixty in under thirty seconds.

"Yes, oh God, yes." She cried out as the inferno swirling in her stomach gained energy and spun outward.

Before she erupted, he stopped abruptly, holding her off. "We can't have you coming too soon. You've waited a long time for this. We need to make it count."

"I appreciate your concern and consideration, but I'm not only on the edge of losing control of my orgasm, I'm about to lose my damn mind."

His laughter filled her chest as she sifted her fingers through his hair, grasped the ends, and tugged. Fumbling around blind, she found his bottom lip, clamped down with her teeth, and pulled.

One of his hands clasped the back of her neck and held her still as his mouth angled over hers and he took control of the kiss. His tongue swept the roof of her mouth, stroked her tongue, then brushed her bottom lip. He slowed the pace and gentled the kiss, and when she'd eased away from the climactic ledge, he rocked his hips and nudged her toward the drop-off once again.

He palmed her breast, rolled her nipple between his thumb and forefinger, and alternated his strokes with Lucas's. Lights flickered behind her eyelids, then grew in intensity, as did the whirling in her stomach. But like last time, he stopped seconds before she exploded.

"Kevin, please."

"You want to stop now? You don't want more?" Before she could answer, he pressed his fingers against her lips. Her mouth instinctively opened wide and drew them in with a strong suck. "Mmmm... I'd say you do want more. Two of us isn't enough, huh? You want to suck off my friend, too?"

His rough, gravelly voice drove her on and she sucked his fingers, imagining them to be his friend's cock. Where this incredibly wild streak came from, she didn't know. She also didn't care. She sank deeper into the fantasy while stroking his fingers with her tongue, drawing them in and out, like she would a man.

She hit a frenzied state, wild and out of control, propelled to the edge of the cliff, with no chance of stopping or turning back. She screamed and bucked wildly as the force of the orgasm ripped through her. Her stomach and pelvic muscles contracted, drawing the men in farther, her skin tingled, and she was lost to everything except the men filling her and the relentless waves of pleasure pulsing through her.

Three more pounding thrusts and Kevin barked a curse, then spasmed with his own climax.

Boneless, barely able to breathe, incapable of speech, with her hands still bound behind his neck, the only thing she could do was collapse onto his chest. When she finally collected herself enough to speak, she said, "See… I need to see you."

"Just a second…" Kevin shifted and twisted and fumbled around like he was looking for something on the bed. "Say goodnight, Lucas."

"I've had a lovely time, Samantha." He spoke from somewhere on her left, and in her relaxed, post-coital state, where everything was sharper and more focused, she realized his voice came through a speaker of some sort, presumably Kevin's phone. "Thanks for letting me join the two of you."

Kevin shifted and what felt like straps around her legs loosened, and the plug or dildo or whatever he'd used was removed. "You and Kevin should come to the club and the three of us can play there sometime."

She wasn't sure what that meant, but considering they'd just had sex, sorta, she figured she needed to at least acknowledge him in some way. "Thank you?" *How exactly did one thank a stranger for… phone sex?*

His kind laughter rang out as Kevin said, "Thanks, man. Shut the door on your way out."

The sound of footsteps echoed through the room and a door—not her door—opened and closed, and they were alone in the silence.

Kevin slipped the blindfold off and brushed her hair away from her face. Holding her cheeks in his palms, he murmured, "Hey."

She still wasn't clear on the details, but Kevin certainly managed to make the fantasy very real, almost too real at times, and emotions threatened to overwhelm her. She couldn't believe he'd gone to so much effort for her, and words eluded her.

Rather than speaking, she lowered her head and kissed him. Not hard and passionate like earlier. The purpose of this kiss was to convey how much she appreciated all he'd done for her and Michaela through-out the weekend, all he'd done for her tonight, and how much she cared for him—despite her desire to keep him at a distance.

When she broke the kiss, he said, "Let's take those cuffs off and get you cleaned up."

Once basic cleanup was completed, Sam curled against Kevin's side and reached for the sheet to pull over them. What she found, instead, was an unfamiliar shirt. She pressed it to her face and drew in a deep breath until she grew dizzy, enjoying the spicy scent. "Lucas's?"

Kevin's eyes narrowed as she took another couple of deep breaths, and finally, having had enough, he snatched it from her hand and tossed it across the room.

She laughed and rested her head on his chest. "So who is Lucas? And how did you pull that off?"

He looked at her through the fringe of his eyelashes, his dark eyes filled with affection… and arrogance. "If I tell you everything, we won't be able to do it again." He glanced to the ceiling. "We're definitely putting a mirror up there before next time."

"What did he mean about coming to the club?"

"Lucas owns a kink club here in town. I've done some work for him and we've gotten to be friends."

"You called him Master Lucas. He's a Dom?"

Kevin chuckled. "He is a Dom and is called Master Lucas by those in the lifestyle. But I'm not in the lifestyle, and I'm not one of his girls, so I refuse to call him that unless he has me in a headlock. I do it mostly just to yank his chain, though."

When she didn't say anything, he jiggled her shoulder with the arm wrapped protectively around her. "What's on your mind?"

Sexual adventures were new to her. Only since her divorce had she felt the freedom to explore. And she often confused herself about what she wanted. "Sometimes, I think I'd like to try some of those things, but I don't know that I'd be any good at it, and I'm not sure that's what I really want. Like the threesome. I liked the idea of the fantasy, but when I thought a strange man was in my bedroom with you, I freaked out."

He stared into space, deep in thought. After a moment, he said, "I don't do well with boxes and labels, so I don't think I could ever say I'm this or that. But we can experiment all you want. Here or, if you're in an adventurous mood, we can go to the club."

The idea of going to a club where there were other people around left her feeling much as she had when Kevin first arrived—terrified and excited at the same time.

"We can play around and try new things, keep what works and toss what doesn't. I've played with Lucas's sub at the club." He grinned broadly. "She also happens to be his wife. And I enjoyed certain aspects. I liked spanking her." His eyes darkened and grew intensely focused on her. "But I enjoyed it a hell of a lot more with you. I fed off your energy and the scene was hotter and more intense than anything I did with Loralei. Does that mean I'm a sadist or need to spank you all the time? No. But it's fun to try different things."

He shifted so he could see her better. "I guess what I'm saying is this… I'll try anything you're up for. Here or at the club. If it works, we can keep it. If not, we say we tried and leave it be. Deal?"

She had a drawer full of toys she played with alone, and the prospect of sharing them with someone else had her shaking her head in agreement before her mind could come up with a list of reasons why this plan was a bad idea.

"Did you just con me into seeing you on a regular basis?"

His grin was wicked, his laugh genuine. "I believe I did."

Chapter Eighteen

Kevin spent the rest of the night wrapped up with Sam in her bed, sleeping as soundly as he'd ever slept. At least until five-thirty when the alarm pulled him from an amazing dream, which turned out to be true, and Sam shooed him out the door like an unwanted burglar.

He and Marianne agreed they'd be foolish not to scoop Sam up while they had the chance, so he ran the idea by Sam before they went to sleep. She was interested, although concerned their personal relationship might interfere with their professional one. He tried to reassure her they would be able to run the two concurrently, but also made sure she understood, even if their personal relationship went down the shitter, her job would be secure. Working out the final details was the last step.

He'd needed to stop by the Vanguard subdivision and Bellamy project on his way to work, so they'd pushed their meeting with Marianne back to eleven. Even at that, he was running thirty minutes late and hoped Marianne and Sam had started hammering out the fine print without him.

Something round and shiny sitting on the lower step caught his attention as he crossed the lot to the front door of Mazze Builder's Myrtle Beach headquarters. He squinted, trying for better focus, and this time it actually worked. His step faltered as he made out the mud pie—white stones, like Sam had at the base of her gutters, ringing the outer edge and larger flat stones forming a K in the middle. Michy must've made it for him last night, or this morning before school, and Sam brought it when she came for their meeting.

Tears stung the back of his eyes as he knelt down and picked up the tin pan as carefully as he would the little treasure who made it. *Dio,* he loved that little girl. He sank down as he struggled to understand his feelings. How could he love someone he'd only recently met?

Regardless of the hows or whys, the facts remained the same. He loved Michaela as much as he loved Spencer, which, he supposed, meant he loved her like his own. And her mamma? He glanced over his shoulder to Marianne's office window.

Yeah, he'd fallen in love with her mamma too.

Things with Sam wouldn't be easy. Time and patience would be necessary to make her understand he wasn't like the other men in her life. He would treat her with kindness and respect and love her with all his heart. Hopefully, over time, she would realize he was the real deal and wouldn't let her down.

The sound of crunching gravel drew his attention to the entry gate. He blinked once, twice, a third time and still, the scene remained the same—horrifying.

In all the time they'd dated, Lizbeth had never made the three-and-a-half-hour trip to Myrtle Beach. She'd never been to his home, and she sure as hell had never been interested in seeing his place of business. How had she found him? More importantly, what the hell was she doing here?

He tried to reach her all day yesterday and she hadn't returned a single call. After getting the *we're done* message, she shows up?

On the same day Sam sat in his office.

Panic ripped through him, seizing his brain like an engine without oil. Survival instincts kicked in and propelled him off the steps and toward her car, cutting her off before she exited.

"What the hell are you doing here?"

She wore large, Hollywood-style sunglasses, but even though they hid most of her face, her red lips and nose and puffy face indicated she'd been crying. A lot.

"Miranda doesn't want to get married. The wedding, their engagement… everything is off."

Relief at hearing her presence was about Wade and Miranda, not the two of them, caused him to let his guard down. As he worked to switch gears and process this new information, he stumbled backward, away from her car.

Taking advantage of his retreat, Lizbeth slung her door open, and, despite the mud pie in his hand, flung herself at him. He palmed the pan and shot his arm out to the side, protecting the precious pie and preventing them from being accessorized with mud.

She wrapped her arms around his neck and buried her face in his chest. Through her sobs, she said, "She met some guy a few months back and has been seeing him on the side. She said she's too young to get married and doesn't want to settle for Wade."

None of this came as a surprise, and while it sucked she waited until two weeks before the wedding to have her revelation, it was much better than after they were married. However, that wasn't his concern at the moment. He needed to get rid of Lizbeth. Now.

"Okay, Lizbeth, calm down." He tried to put some distance between them, but she clung to him for dear life.

"What am I going to do?"

Get back in the fucking car and follow me out of this lot. Hell, even if he only managed to get her back into the car, it would be infinitely better than her glued to his front like a papoose.

"Lizbeth, get in the car. Let's go somewhere else and talk."

While she rambled about everything being ruined—not just Wade and Miranda's wedding, but her career as well—he eased her back toward the open car door. "Get in the car."

"Please, please don't do this."

As the pleading words continued to trail from her mouth, the hair on the back of his neck stood on end. He didn't have to turn around to know Sam had made an appearance on the steps behind him. The alarm shredding through him was proof enough.

He peeled Lizbeth off and spun around, praying his gut instincts were wrong.

They were never wrong, and he found not only Sam, but Marianne standing on the steps, shock and dismay registering on their faces.

Oblivious to the audience—or uncaring—Lizbeth continued with the dramatics. "I've put so much into this wedding, and Mother and Daddy have already paid for everything." Even though he stood at an angle to her, she fisted the front of his shirt and shook him, trying to regain his attention. "Please work this out with me and help me through this disaster. I need you more than ever. Don't quit on me now."

Her words acted like jabs to the gut, each one knocking a little more breath out of him until no oxygen remained and his heart barely beat. The agonizing gasp and despair twisting Sam's beautiful face was the final blow that practically cut his legs out from under him.

With a harsh grip on Lizbeth's arm, he jerked her off him and turned to Sam. "Please let me explain."

She wrapped her arms around her stomach as if the pain threatened to tear her apart and she needed to hold herself together. Without saying a word, she struggled down the steps, then walked across the gravel lot to her car. She didn't limp—she was too fucking proud for that—but the flinch around her eyes and mouth, as well as the tightening of her shoulders, showed how much each step cost.

Still holding his precious pie in hand, he reached her car at the same time as her. "Please, Sam, hear me out."

She stared him straight in the eye, anger, despair... hatred filling her expression. "Are you still involved with her?"

"No." Thank God he'd gone to Riverside to end things. Even though Lizbeth had avoided him, he'd left a message and could answer Sam honestly and without hesitation. "Things with us have been over for a while..."

Mother fucker! The second the words left his mouth he wanted to snatch them back. He sounded just like her ex-husband, something Sam would tweak to immediately.

"Did she know it was over?"

Fuck! Fuck, fuck, fuck.

There were all kinds of ways to justify the situation or bullshit his way around the truth. Yes, Lizbeth had to know they'd reached the end of the line, same as him. But since he hadn't broached the subject, neither had she, and they'd maintained the status quo.

And that's what Sam was looking for. Bottom line, he hadn't officially ended his relationship with Lizbeth before he started seeing Sam. Jesus, he didn't want to tell the truth and hurt her further, but he didn't have a choice.

He closed his eyes so he didn't see the disgust in her face and shook his head. "No."

The mud pie caught him squarely in the chest with enough force to know she'd sent it flying with quite a punch. "Don't ever come near me or my daughter again."

"Sam, please. In the name of everything holy, don't do this. Let me explain."

She shook her head and bit down hard on her bottom lip. "I've heard everything I need to." She slammed her car door shut, revved the engine, and roared out of the lot.

As the pie dripped onto his pants, he fought the urge to draw the plate to him, using it to fill the gaping hole left in his chest by Sam's departure. He turned and caught sight of a bewildered Lizbeth and a highly pissed-off Marianne. He couldn't remember ever feeling this kind of deep, aching grief where every fiber of his being ached and cried out in wrenching pain.

He needed to put as much distance between himself and everyone else as possible. It was entirely probable he would completely burst from the pain and no one needed to lay witness to that kind of destruction.

He pivoted on his heel and walked to the end of the lot, circled the back of the office building, and headed toward the shop. Everyone was out on a job, so the shop would be empty. He could sit in there and mourn his loss without any interference.

"Kevin." Footsteps pounded behind him. "Kevin."

Fury swelled within him and he struggled to keep it contained, rather than turn and take it out on Lizbeth. He wanted to be angry with her and blame her for everything, but it wasn't her fault. He had no one to blame but himself.

"Not now, Lizbeth. For your sake, leave me alone."

Stopping to unlock the shop door slowed him down long enough for her to catch up. "Who was that?"

The only thing preventing him from losing his shit and committing murder was Lizbeth's tone. She didn't sound angry, or even hurt. She sounded concerned. He lifted his gaze to hers and was surprised to find she'd removed her sunglasses and was searching his face for answers, truly concerned about him and not herself for a change. The soft, caring hand she rested on his shoulder backed up the concern in her eyes.

"Please talk to me. Who is she?"

"That," he said, swinging the door open, "was my life."

Lizbeth drew in a deep breath and swallowed hard. "I've known for a long time I wasn't the one for you, but I tried to put off the inevitable as long as possible." She stepped into the shop behind him and glanced around. Greasy rags lay on the counters. Five-gallon buckets were stacked all around. Whiffs of gas and oil mixed with sawdust and filled the air with a stench he found calming.

A stench Lizbeth struggled to breathe through. Rather than turn and run from the building, she searched under the workbench and found an old, metal barstool. After shifting around and getting as comfortable as possible, she said, "I'm sorry you're hurting. I'm also sorry for my part in that. Will you tell me about her?"

Sam spent the rest of the day trying—unsuccessfully—to get her head on straight. No matter what she did, where she stopped, who she spoke with, she thought of Kevin. The worst came when she closed her eyes to try and contain her pounding headache. The second her eyes closed, Kevin's face appeared, just as he'd been last night, nose to nose with her, asking, *"Do you trust me?"*

Anger and hurt, at him as well as herself, made her skin feel like it would boil off. She should've read the warning signs—the constant phones calls, easily explained away as Lizilla—but she hadn't. Maybe she'd just refused to examine things too closely for fear of what she'd find.

The ringing doorbell made her jump and she nearly launched her pizza right off her plate. She hadn't been up for cooking—turns out she wasn't into eating, either—so she'd taken the easy way out and ordered pizza. Michy had been thrilled to have pizza twice in one week, so the arrangement worked well for both of them.

She set the plate and untouched slice on the coffee table and limped to the door. An Angelina Jolie lookalike with dark eyes and gorgeous black hair stood on the stoop. Lizilla was supermodel gorgeous—exactly the kind of woman she envisioned Kevin with. The two of them certainly made more sense than he and Sam. Faced with the full reality of the situation, a fresh wave of anger and hurt pressed against her chest and nearly buckled her knees.

Not seeing a need to play dumb—she'd played that part for long enough—she said, "You're Lizbeth."

The Angelina lookalike smiled, not in an evil I'm-going-to-cut-your-heart-out way, but with soft sympathy. "I am."

Before Sam dove into the apologies and explanations, Michy ran to the door, curious about their visitor. She skidded to a stop, eyes wide, mouth hanging open. She didn't know who Angelina Jolie was, so she probably thought the princess from *Beauty and the Beast* had landed on her doorstep. "Wooowww… Who are you?"

Lizbeth flashed a movie star-worthy smile that made Samantha feel like a troll. As she knelt to eye level with Michy, Sam found herself wanting to grab her long, flowing top and hold it off the ground so she didn't get dirty. "Hi there. You must be Michaela."

Michy's eyes widened farther as amazement and wonder lit her expression. Turning back to the Angie double, she whispered, "How'd you know?"

"I'm a friend of Kevin's, and he's told me all about you."

Michy's eyes lit up and she hopped on one foot, like Tigger bouncing on his tail. "He did? What'd he say?"

"Let's see…" She tapped a perfectly manicured nail against her chin and looked up, thinking. "You go to afterschool with Spencer, your favorite book is *The Poky Little Puppy,* and you make the world's best pancakes."

Michy giggled and bounced harder. "Yep. Kevin taught me." Another couple of hops. "What else did he say? Did he tell you about my mommy, too?"

"Okay," Sam said, grabbing Michy by the shoulders to spin her around toward the living room. "That's enough questions. Go watch Dora."

Michy skipped off and Lizbeth stood to face Sam, her smile still intact. "He told me quite a bit about you, too."

God Almighty, did the man not have a caring bone in his body? Why would he talk to his girlfriend about the woman he'd been cheating with? She never would've believed him to be this big of an ass, but once again, she'd proven to be the world's worst judge of character.

"I had no idea—"

Lizbeth threw up a hand to cut her off. "Please, don't. May I come in for a moment?"

Dread sank in Sam's gut at having this confrontation, but she couldn't shut the door on Lizbeth and deprive her of the opportunity to say her piece. Unlike Sheila, Sam hadn't realized Kevin was involved with someone else. There hadn't been pictures of Lizbeth lying around while she and Kevin screwed each other's brains out, but that didn't change the facts. Lizbeth deserved the chance to say all the things Sam wished she'd said to Sheila.

She nodded and stepped to the side, allowing Lizbeth to enter. "Let's go into the kitchen." She didn't want Michy to hear her mom get cussed out, but also, for some stupid reason, she didn't want Michy knowing Kevin was a worthless, lowlife, scum-sucking jerk. The least she could do was allow her daughter to hold on to a little of her hero worship, so she wouldn't be completely devastated.

Lizbeth followed her into the kitchen, looking around as they went. Their house was small and filled with well-used furniture, but it was neat and clean and the best Sam could provide. Even though she believed Lizbeth came from money and lived in a luxurious condo somewhere, she refused to be self-conscious or embarrassed about their home.

Her personal temple, however, was another matter. As she stood in Lizbeth's shadow, she was excruciatingly self-conscious about her height, weight, and overall shortcomings. She skimmed her gaze over Lizbeth's chest and a small flutter of satisfaction rippled through her. At least she had Lizbeth soundly beat in the boob department.

"I'm sorry," she tried again. "I never would've gotten involved with Kevin had I known—"

"I didn't come here for an apology," Lizbeth said, once again cutting off Sam's defense. "If anything, I should be the one apologizing."

"What?" Sam's breath left in a whoosh. Had Kevin somehow brainwashed this woman into believing she was at fault?

Lizbeth pulled out a chair and started to sit. "May I?"

"Ummm…" Sam scratched the side of her head, then tossed up a hand in defeat. "Sure. Can I get you something to drink?"

Lizbeth's eyes crinkled at the corners as she laughed. "Kevin said it would be pointless to come here. But you haven't tossed me out yet and even offered a drink. I've gotten much further than he thought I would."

Okay, so maybe some of what Kevin said about Lizbeth was true. He'd given the impression she'd lost her mind, and Sam had to agree with him, at least on that point. She crossed her arms over her stomach and leaned against the counter. "If you're not here for an apology or to rip me to shreds for trying to steal your man, why are you here?"

"I want you to give Kevin another chance."

"You really are crazy." The words escaped before she could stop them, and heat crawled around her neck. "I'm sorry, I didn't… Well, I sort of did mean it."

Lizbeth's laugh was deep and husky… and genuine.

What the hell?

Sam ran a hand over her forehead and wondered if she'd made a mistake and let a madwoman into her home.

"Kevin was never my man. We've dated off and on for a while, but he never cared for me the way he does for you. He never looked at me the way he did while talking about you." She glanced toward the opening of the living room and her eyes misted over. "He's absolutely smitten with Michaela and will be devastated if he loses the two of you."

Her shoulders sagged and she swallowed hard. "The only time I've ever seen Kevin upset was when his friend, Kat, was injured in a serious accident a year and a half ago. He was beside himself, sick with fear for her and Erik, and filled with anguish of all they would lose if Kat didn't recover." A single tear streaked down her cheek as she swallowed. "He showed the same grief-stricken expression today as you drove away."

Sam's lungs seized, forcing her to consciously draw air in and out. She wanted to believe Lizbeth spoke the truth—why would she lie?—but she had a hard time understanding why he would talk to Lizbeth about the woman he cheated with.

"I'm so sorry your hurt has been compounded by him talking about me. He cheated on you, and then he had the audacity to cry to you about losing me?"

Lizbeth shook her head and patted the table. "Please sit and talk with me."

Sitting was better than sliding to the floor, which she feared might happen at any moment, so she pulled out the chair and planted her ass.

"Kevin wanted out of our relationship for a long time."

"Then why didn't he get out?" What was it with men? They wanted out of relationships, but they didn't have the balls to say so. Cowards.

Lizbeth fiddled with a button on her blouse. "Sometimes I feel like an old maid who will never find the right guy to settle down with. Kevin and I weren't right for each other permanently, but being with someone is better than being alone. He's such a nice guy. I knew he wouldn't dump me before the wedding, especially with both of us in the wedding party. To further hedge my bets, I convinced my sister to have the wedding at Kevin's. She wanted an outdoor wedding, and his house on the river is the perfect setting. But I wanted the wedding there for personal gain."

It certainly sounded as if Lizbeth had gone to a lot of trouble to trap Kevin, but he was a grown man who could've ended things if he wanted. At some point, one has to take responsibility for their own happiness and stand their ground. Even if it means being unkind.

"He still should've ended things with you before…," she waved her hand awkwardly, "…me."

"He tried. He told me on Sunday to expect him on Monday, that we needed to talk. His intent was clear, so I went to Raleigh and refused to take his calls."

"That was still after he and I… got together."

"Tell me something. How aggressively did Kevin pursue you?"

"He didn't. Not at all. It started out by the kids arranging to meet at the Boardwalk. I fell and hurt my ankle, and Kevin invited us back to his place so the kids could swim, and I would have help with Michy. I'm not defending him. It just didn't start out as anything but friendship."

Lizbeth smiled and nodded once, then raised her brows and gave Sam a *go on* look.

She thought back to what happened next. Kevin carrying her to the backyard… wanting to kiss her, but holding himself back…

When she performed her pseudo-striptease, he'd been hot and cold, interested but upset. She'd been confused by his mixed signals, but now she understood. He was attracted, but hadn't wanted to be. He'd tried to be the gentleman, to keep his distance, but…

"I was the pursuer," she said quietly. She snapped her gaze to Lizbeth's. "I misunderstood something Wade said and had the impression Kevin was free. He didn't respond to my advances until…" He found her toy box.

Lizbeth smiled knowingly. "Kevin's a man. He's built like a brick shit house—"

Samantha laughed at the potty word coming from Lizbeth's perfect crimson mouth.

"—but he's only so strong. He already knew in his heart I wasn't the one. I suspect he also knew, even then, that you are."

"He should've been upfront and told me in the beginning about you."

Lizbeth nodded thoughtfully. "When was the beginning?"

Sam took a deep breath before dropping her head onto her folded arms. *When was the beginning?* At the job site when she started making plans to seduce him? At the beach when he was being helpful? As he carried her to the backyard and almost kissed her, but didn't?

That would've been the optimum time, or when she'd been doing her lawn chair striptease.

But he hadn't and things progressed, and now, here she sat with his girlfriend, ex-girlfriend, *whatever,* listening to what a great guy he was and how she should give him a second chance.

Lizbeth took a deep breath, as if to speak, but didn't.

"Go ahead," Sam said, looking up. "Why stop now?"

Lizbeth played with the fringe on her handbag, still unsure. "I understand you've..." She paused and pressed her lips together. "I don't have specifics, but I know you've been hurt in the past. Kevin is furious with himself for being no better than the others who let you down."

Pressure built in Sam's chest as emotion clogged her throat.

"If he didn't want to hurt me, someone he marginally cares about, can you imagine how distraught he is about hurting you, someone he loves?"

Sam shook her head. "He doesn't love me."

Lizbeth smiled as she pushed to her feet and gathered her bag. "Please think about what I've said."

Sam sat in the chair, numb and unable to move, as she watched Lizbeth's retreating back.

Someone he loves.

Did he love her? Did she love him? The better question was did she *want* to love him?

She'd sworn to never get seriously involved with anyone again. She'd started this thing with Mazze as a sexual game, no attachments, simply a now-and-then bed partner. She hadn't meant to fall for him. It just happened...

Her breath left in a whoosh as she recalled his defensive words regarding Michael.

"Sometimes, it's not always that black and white. Sometimes, things happen, even when people don't set out to hurt those they care about."

She'd been furious with his defense of Michael, but now she understood his intent. He wasn't defending Michael, but himself.

As much as she hated to admit it, he was kind of right. She just conceded to doing the same thing. She hadn't intended to fall in love; it just happened.

With a deep breath and trembling hands, she picked up her cell and dialed his number.

He answered on the first ring, his voice filled with anxious hopefulness. "Hey."

Hearing his voice set squirrels loose, scurrying out of control around her belly. She locked down on her emotional reaction and kept her focus on her reason for calling.

"I have one question for you."

After a long pause, he said, "Okay." Hopefulness evaporated, anxiety remained.

"I accept responsibility for being the pursuer. I misunderstood something Wade said and thought you were available. But at the pool on Saturday, when I came on to you, why didn't you stop me?"

His breath left in a rush of muttered Italian.

"If there is any chance of us working this out, you won't lie to me. You won't even think about lying to me."

He ejected another curse before his voice grew soft and reverent, as if praying. "You're the most beautiful woman in the world to me, and sexy as hell. You don't seem to see yourself the same way, though. You watched me from the corner of your eye, like you were unsure and needed to reaffirm my interest. I didn't stop you, because I didn't want to give you any reason to be insecure."

"So I was a pity fuck?"

"What? No! Shit."

He sounded so distraught; she couldn't help but laugh.

"You had my attention the moment you slammed your hands onto your hips and your shirt pulled tight, showing perfect creamy cleavage that made my mouth water."

Without thought, she reached down and gathered the sides of her blouse.

"I was dying to see your eyes, to know their color." She pictured him pacing back and forth, rubbing his neck. "I prayed for the strength to get through two weeks, to get the fucking wedding behind me so I could end things with Lizbeth. I didn't mean for anyone to get hurt. Hell, I was trying to make sure no one got hurt. I screwed up." He took another long pause and released a deep exhale. "I'm sorry, Sam. I'm so damned sorry."

That she believed. The crack of his voice and the desperate unspoken plea for forgiveness nearly broke her resolve. But she had some thinking to do and other issues she needed to work through before she made a decision about Kevin. This situation with him made her realize how much angry bitterness toward Michael and her brothers she still harbored. She wasn't sure she could forgive Kevin, but she'd never be able to move forward with him, or anyone else, until she forgave the hurts of the past.

"I have some thinking to do. Is the job offer still open, regardless of what happens with us personally?"

"Absolutely. Please, please take the job. Marianne is threatening to feed me to the alligators for screwing that up." His voice took on his normal light, teasing tone, but then grew sad again. "Regardless of what you decide about me, Mazze Builders is a strong, solid company and will be around for a long time. We'll take care of you and Michaela and would be honored to have you work with us."

As he talked, the emotion filling her chest expanded and began to overflow. When he finished speaking, she... the one who never, ever cried, wiped a tear from her cheek.

"Tell Marianne I'll let her know something by the end of the week."

Chapter Nineteen

*A*fter hanging up the phone with Kevin and getting Michy into bed, Sam made her way to the bathtub where she cried her way through bouts of anger, despair, grief, and back to rage. She soaked so long, she needed to drain the cold water and refill three times. Despite all her losses over the past several years, she hadn't cried since her dad's funeral.

When her family liquidated the business and sold off everything she and her dad built, she went into shock. When shit hit the fan with Michael, she numbed to everything, and after the numbness wore off, she refused to shed a single tear over his worthless, cheating, lying ass.

Once the stockpiled tears started falling, she experienced the mother of all cleansings. Emotionally exhausted, she expected to collapse into a deep sleep, but as she crawled into bed—where Kevin's scent surrounded her and she found reminders of their time together everywhere—sleep eluded her. By two, she'd come to the conclusion she might need to burn her bedroom furniture and start all over.

At three, she gave up and moved to the couch, where she managed to sleep in ten and fifteen minute spurts. Enough to make her miserable, not enough to count toward any real rest. At four, she got her cell and dialed Michael. He and Sheila disrupted her entire life, so she found it difficult to feel bad about costing them a few hours of sleep.

After twenty minutes, she learned that, if she believed Michael, Sheila had been the pursuer. Feeling neglected by Sam, he succumbed to Sheila's advances on an overnight business trip to Charlotte. He wasn't sorry the affair happened and wouldn't change anything.

Her next phone call went out to idiot brother number one, Trey.

"Sam, what's wrong?"

They hadn't spoken since Christmas, so it made sense he would automatically assume something was wrong. Also, four forty-five a.m. phone calls usually meant a family emergency.

"I need to ask you some questions."

Sheets rustled as he moved around. "Now? In the middle of the night?"

"It's early morning, not the middle of the night. Why did you think I couldn't run Seymore Builders?"

Betty's voice in the background accompanied more rustling and a groan as he crawled out of bed. "This can't wait until morning? Real morning?"

"No."

There was a squeak, like a door opening and closing. "We just didn't think you could do it alone." His voice echoed, and she assumed he'd gone to the shitter… the perfect place for him to have this conversation.

"I worked there my entire life and knew the business inside and out, nearly as well as Dad."

"You constantly ran things by him and never made any decisions by yourself—"

"I made all of my own decisions. I never had less than three projects going at one time, with a million small decisions to make throughout the day. We also had big-picture decisions to make, and those we talked out. After gathering information, we made our own decisions. It's called brainstorming, dickwad."

After a long pause, he said, "Sorry, Sam, we did what we thought was best for everyone."

"No, you all did what you thought was best for *you*. You saw a chance to sell everything off and make a pile of money."

"Mom's the only one who benefited from any of the money." His voice grew tight, defensive.

"Really? You didn't take a fee for all of your time? How much has the initial investment grown? Even in this shitty market, I bet the total value has increased. Am I right?"

"I don't like what you're implying."

"Tough. Shit. I haven't liked anything you've done for a long time. Like me, you'll get over it."

She disconnected but decided to give her mother the courtesy of not calling until six. She took a shower and dressed and tried to eat breakfast, but nothing sounded promising, so she gave up and sat at the kitchen table while watching the clock. When the big hand hit twelve and the little hit six, she picked up the phone.

Her mother answered much the same as the others. "Sam? What's wrong?"

"I'm trying to work through some things, and I need your help."

After a brief pause, her mother said, "Okay."

"Why did you agree to sell off everything? Did you really believe I wasn't capable of running Seymore Builders without Daddy?"

This time, the pause was long enough to cause a truckload of tension to build in Sam's gut. Her daddy always said, *"Never ask the question if you don't want the answer."* This would be the perfect scenario to heed caution, but she needed answers. Good, bad, ugly… whatever the response, she wanted to understand why her mom sided with her brothers and left Sam out in the cold.

"You were more than capable of running the business."

Sam gasped, more confused than before. "Then why did you sell everything out from under me?"

"I watched your dad spend many sleepless nights, watching the weather forecast, waiting to see if the wind would blow hard enough to dry the ground, wondering if the loan would come through or if the sale would happen in time to pay off the loan without accruing penalties.

"I wouldn't have chosen that life for you, so after your dad died—of a heart attack from the stress—and your brothers approached me about selling, I agreed. Not because I doubted you, but because I wanted to protect you. You had Michael and Michaela, and what I thought was a wonderful life. I wanted you free of the stress and aggravation that came with the business."

Sam was speechless. Her mother should've allowed Sam the choice, but she'd acted out of love and responsibility as a mother, protecting her daughter. Sam cut her eyes to the bedroom… Much the way Sam tried to protect Michaela from harm.

"Why didn't you tell me?"

Her mother sighed. "I tried. You were so angry; you wouldn't listen. After things fell apart with Michael, I realized my mistake. But it was too late. Everything was gone." She paused to take a deep, shaky breath. "I could've taken the money and put you back into business, but I still didn't think it was the best choice for you, especially not as a single mom, so I left well enough alone."

Sam's head was reeling. She'd gotten the response she expected from Michael and Trey, but her mother's explanation left her ungrounded and flailing.

"Why did you need these answers now, sweetheart, at six o'clock in the morning?"

Sam and her mom weren't as close as Sam had been to her dad, but in a house full of men, the two had needed to stick together to keep from losing their minds. She told her mom about Kevin and all that transpired over the past few days, at least the G-rated mom version, and then waited for her response.

The response was slow in coming, and she could tell her mom carefully considered her words before speaking. "Sometimes, people make bad decisions with the best of intentions."

"Yeah." Sometimes people made decisions without thought to others, like Michael and Trey. Sometimes, people like her mom… and Kevin… made bad choices while trying to do good.

"I'm sorry for calling so early. Thanks for talking to me and clearing all this up for me." She brushed her hair away from her face and massaged her temple. "I'm sorry I didn't listen before when you tried to explain. I guess I wasn't ready to hear it."

She disconnected the call as Michy bounced into the kitchen, ready for breakfast. One look at Sam, and her bounce thudded to a halt. "What's wrong, Mommy?"

Sam took a deep breath and opened her arms, needing her sweet, innocent baby girl close to her. "Nothing."

"But you've been crying. You never cry. Not even when you gots hurt."

"Yeah, but you know what? It's okay to cry sometimes." She brushed the baby-fine hair curled around Michy's face away from her forehead and gave her a kiss. "I'm fine. Let's get your breakfast and get you to school."

While Michy ate, Sam rummaged around in the bathroom drawers and found the cover-up and foundation she never wore. She dabbed a little on her finger and went to work on the dark circles hanging below her red, swollen eyes. Combined with the pink nose, swollen lips, and puffy face, this was a lost cause. Maybe she should wrap her arm in a bandage, slap a few Band-Aids here and there, and claim assault by a bus. She already had the limp to back up the claim.

She wasn't willing to let Kevin off the hook just yet and still wasn't exactly sure what she intended to say to him. But as far as her life went, regardless of her appearance, she was a hundred pounds lighter and freer than she'd been in a long, long time. She supposed, regardless of what happened with her and Kevin, she had him to thank for her freedom.

Chapter Twenty

*T*he past eighteen hours were the longest of Kevin's life. He couldn't remember ever being so miserable and felt like his soul was slowly and methodically being sliced to pieces. Sam's call last night brought a sliver of hope, but he hadn't heard from her since, and neither had Marianne.

"You going home anytime soon?"

Kevin lifted his head from the easel of his upraised hands and looked across his office at Marianne. Although pissed about the screwed-up work situation with Sam, she understood where he'd been coming from with Lizbeth. She had his back, regardless of how badly he messed up.

He once told Marianne she and Sam were a lot alike. Right now, the only thing keeping him sane was the hope that if Marianne understood his motivations, Sam might also understand. He wasn't sure she would ever forgive him, but if she got to the point of understanding and didn't hate him… that would be a million times better than where they were now.

"Yeah, I suppose. I've been here all day and haven't accomplished a god-damned thing. No need to keep spinning my wheels with more of the same."

"I'm sorry it went down like this. I never thought I'd see the day my big brother fell in love…" She dropped her head and sighed, then looked up at him with a mischievous expression. "Maybe she'll take this job, and your charm will eventually win her back."

"God, I hope so." Especially since hope was the only thing he had at this point.

He helped Marianne shut down the office and walked her to her car. "In the spirit of positive thinking," he said, "I'm going home and making a pitcher of sweet iced tea."

He told Sam he wouldn't disappoint her again by not having any on hand. He would keep a damned pitcher of sweet tea in his fridge forever… just in case.

Two hours later, Kevin had made the tea, poured out all the alcohol in the house so he wasn't tempted to revert to his old coping mechanisms, and managed to cook a halfway decent dinner. He'd just gone to the bedroom and stripped off his shirt when a knock sounded at the door.

Hope drove his heart to pump triple time, but he forced himself to take a deep breath and run through the list of possible visitors, so he wasn't crushed when he found someone other than Sam at his door. He'd tried to call Callie earlier to ask a few questions about the furnishings in the Vanguard sales office. Maybe she decided to drop by, rather than call. His visitor might also be Wade.

The poor guy was as annihilated as Kevin. He came to work this morning, but when Kevin dropped by to check on him, he was such a mess Kevin sent him home. Although, he doubted Wade actually went home. The more likely scenario was he'd headed to Riverside to try and change Miranda's mind, or to kill the son of a bitch she'd been messing around with.

Hello? Pot… meet kettle.

As he rounded the corner, the most beautiful sight in the world greeted him. Well past her bedtime, Michy stood beside her mom, a mud pie in her hands, the sweetest smile in the world on her face. Her mamma appeared less sweet, a whole lot wary, and nervous.

He wanted to go straight to Sam, but Michy was the one bearing gifts, so he knelt in front of her and tried to control the crack in his voice. "Hey, *piccolina,* what cha got there?"

"Mommy said she messed up your other pie, so she helped me make this one for you."

Sam and Michaela were so much stronger than him, because despite his best effort, he couldn't hold back the tears stinging his eyes. Sam would never have helped Michy make this pie, let alone take her anywhere near him, if she didn't intend to at least hear him out.

He ran a hand over his face to wipe the struggling tears away and lifted the pie from her hands. "Thank you. You don't know how much this means to me." He wrapped his arm around her and held her tightly, then kissed her forehead and stood. To Sam, he said, "Will you come in?"

He realized she also had a tear in her eye, and the sight completely unraveled him. "Yeah, for a minute. I need to get Michy to bed."

He set the pie on the kitchen counter while Michy ran off to the living room and changed the channel on the TV.

Sam laughed nervously. "I guess she's making herself at home."

"Yeah…" He smiled as she climbed onto the couch and wrapped up in the blanket he kept on the back of the sofa. Nothing in the world would make him happier than to have these two part of his home. He cleared his throat and nodded to the pie. "Thank you. I don't know how or where, but I'll keep it forever."

An awkward silence filled the room while they stared at each other, each trying to read the others' thoughts. When he couldn't stand the silence anymore, he said, "I screwed up. I'm so sorry."

He had the sense he should try to explain again, but what more was there for him to say. Lizbeth said their conversation went well, and she'd explained how she used the wedding to manipulate him. She said Sam listened, so she knew the basics. Other than saying he was sorry, again, he was at a loss.

After what seemed like another two hours of standing in a black hole, Sam said, "If you could go back in time and change things, would you?"

"Hell yeah." He glanced to the couch to see if Michy had caught the slip. "I would've ended things with Lizbeth five months ago, wedding or no. If I had still been with her when I met you…" He let the sentence drop off as he thought back to the weekend. "This is where I get tripped up."

He rubbed the back of his neck and paced around the island. "If I'd stopped your advances, I'm not sure we would've picked up again. I wouldn't have had the time with you and Michy, and I wouldn't have fallen in love." He stopped and looked into her eyes, imploring her to understand his dilemma. "It was wrong. But you are the best thing that's ever happened to me. How can I regret that?"

He leaned against a barstool and scrubbed his hands over his face. "I'm human, and I'm a man. We screw up. But I swear to you, I will never willingly or knowingly or intentionally hurt you again. If I think you might not be okay with something, I won't do it. Well,"—he leaned in close, making sure Michy couldn't hear him—"if it's something kinky, and I'm not sure you'll like it, I'll ask, we'll talk about it, and decide together."

She ran her hand up her forehead, brushing loose curls away from her face, and blew out a breath. "Part of me thinks I'm an idiot for even standing here talking to you, and part of me understands sometimes people make mistakes while trying to do the right thing."

Whoa… Lizbeth had actually gotten through to her? He owed her big time.

She must've read the shock on his face because she laughed and said, "Yeah, surprised me, too. After Lizbeth left, I spent a long time thinking about my past, and I made some calls. I called Michael and found out he wouldn't change anything. He's still an asshole. I called my oldest brother, Trey, and got the same response. One more strike and you would've been out. But then I called my mom." She leaned against the kitchen counter and crossed her arms. "She didn't sell the business because she doubted my ability."

"What?"

She nodded. "She sold it because she thought the stress killed my dad, and she didn't want the same thing for me."

"No shit." He shot another quick glance to the sofa, where Michy had fallen asleep. Maybe he could convince her mamma to fall asleep here, too. "Why didn't she tell you?"

She chewed her lip and stared at the floor. "She might've tried, but I was too angry to listen."

Sam didn't look sheepish often, and even though the response was inappropriate, he laughed. "This is a tough business. I understand why she wanted to protect you." He turned serious. "Would she have objections to you being part of a larger team? Not running solo, but working with me and Marianne?"

Although things were looking better than a few hours ago, she still hadn't accepted his apology, nor let him off the hook. If she would agree to working with them, he might be able to use Marianne's tactics and win her over with his charm… without the aggression he used the first time they met.

She swiped her tongue over her bottom lip a few times while considering his question. "I don't know if she would or not. But I want to work in the business again, and I want to work with you and Marianne.

I'll call her tomorrow morning and finalize the details."

He exhaled sharply. *Grazie a Dio.* The relief at having her agree to work with them was tremendous. It was probably foolish to push too hard, too soon, but he needed to know where they stood personally.

He stepped close and hooked his fingers through the belt loops of her jeans. "How do you feel about getting involved with the boss?"

She kept her chin lowered but slowly lifted her gaze to meet his. Her pupils dilated and a flush spread over her neck, up to her cheeks. After a few quick breaths, she said, "Will the boss feed me lunch every day?"

The heat coloring her features jumped to him and set him off like a match. Picking her up in his arms, he checked to make sure Michy was still asleep while carrying Sam to the bedroom. "Sugar, I'll feed you breakfast, lunch, dinner, and a bedtime snack if you'll let me."

She wrapped her arms around his neck and kissed the skin just below his ear. Whispering, she said, "I can live with that benefits package. You have yourself a deal."

Ten Months Later

For the past ten months, Sam and Kevin had been on a slow and steady pace, especially where Michy was concerned. He spent most nights at their house, but with the exception of Saturday and Sunday mornings, he left before Michy woke.

Friday nights were family movie night, complete with pizza and one beer. Saturday was family fun day, which always included Spencer. Sunday was the day of rest where they lay around the house and did absolutely nothing.

Along with allowing him to stay overnight, Sam had also gotten comfortable with letting Kevin sleep in her room without moving to the sofa. He'd gotten used to waking up bright and early when Michy jumped into the middle of the bed with them.

It was Thursday morning, so normally Kevin would be gone when Michy woke, but this morning, for some mysterious reason, she wandered into Sam's room at four a.m.

"What's wrong, sweetie," Sam asked, scooting closer to Kevin so Michy could crawl in next to her.

"I want to sleep with you," Michy said in a sleepy voice, then yawned widely.

At five, Michy patted Sam's hand to wake her again. "Mommy, will you help me make pancakes for Kevin this morning?"

Pancakes? At five? On a Thursday? Sam yawned and stretched as much as she could without waking Kevin. "It's Thursday. We don't get pancakes except Saturday and Sunday."

"I know. But if we start making pancakes for him, maybe he won't leave."

Behind her, Kevin stiffened and drew in a sharp intake of air, while Sam stopped breathing altogether. Whispering, to keep up the ruse of Kevin sleeping, she said, "I don't understand."

"He's only here on the days he makes pancakes. The other mornings he leaves before I get up, but if we make him pancakes, he might not leave."

"Oh, Michy." Sam's chest couldn't ache more if a thousand-pound elephant sat on her. Michy was so much smarter than she gave her credit for. She should've realized she knew Kevin spent every night at their house but left before dawn.

She rolled Michy over to hug her and bit her lip to keep from crying at the tears sparkling in her daughter's eyes. "Sweetie, Kevin doesn't leave or stay because of pancakes." She took a deep breath, then sighed in defeat. "He leaves because I make him."

Michy's face crumpled. "Why?"

Because I'm still trying to protect you... and still doing a lousy job of it.

She brushed a curl away from Michy's forehead and kissed her soft cheek. "I'm a silly mommy that does dumb things sometimes."

Kevin pushed onto his elbow and rested his chin on Sam's shoulder. "I have an idea that might solve all of our problems."

Sam looked at him from the corner of her eye while Michy turned her shiny blue eyes to him.

The corner of his lip kicked up and he appeared nervous. "How about we get married, so we'll always be together."

"What?" Sam gasped while Michy jumped up on the bed and did her best Tigger impression.

"Whoa, *piccolina*," Kevin said, catching her as she lost balance and tumbled over onto them. "Don't get too excited yet. Your mamma hasn't said yes. I caught her a little by surprise."

"A little?" Sam rolled onto her back and ran both hands over her face, wiping away a stray tear as well as the sweat that broke out on her forehead. "How about a lot? We've never even discussed marriage. Other than for me to say I'd never do it again."

Taking her hand in his, he said, "I love you, Sam. We make a great team, both at home and the office. Erik once told me you don't marry the one you can live with; you marry the one you can't live without. I can't imagine living my life without you and Michy... I wouldn't have a life without you two." He kissed her palm. "Please marry me."

Things with them were so easy it almost seemed too good to be true. Nothing about their relationship was strained or tense, like with Michael, and she found herself always waiting for the blowup.

But it had been ten months, and he was right. They were a great team, and she couldn't ask for a better father for Michy. The idea of getting married again terrified her, but she did lots of things with Kevin that scared the crap out of her, starting with the night of the fantasy threesome all the way up until last weekend when they went to the club and he spanked her in front of Lucas.

Life with him was thrilling and sometimes scary, but he always kept his promise to keep her safe and she never doubted his love.

She thought about the night so long ago when Michy ran full-throttle into the kitchen and jumped into Kevin's arms, fully trusting him to catch her. If Michy trusted him so completely, she should too.

"Okay," she said, taking a deep breath. "Do you promise to always catch me?"

His brow wrinkled and a smile played at his lips as he struggled to understand her question. "What?"

"Michy ran into the kitchen one night and took a flying leap into your arms. You weren't expecting it, yet you caught her... just as she expected. Will you always catch me?"

His eyes softened and all the love he had for her shone brightly in their dark depths. "Always, even when I'm the one who pushes you."

It was her turn to look puzzled.

"I won't let your life become dull and boring and mundane." He bent over and spoke into her ear. "Especially in the bedroom. I'll always catch you, but I'll also be the one nudging you off the cliff sometimes."

She wrapped her arms around his neck and nuzzled his nose with hers. "Deal."

Michy, who seemed to understand the importance of this conversation, had taken a seat at the end of the bed and waited for the grownups to talk it out. Sensing the end of the negotiations, she crawled up Sam's legs and sat on her thighs. In a soft voice, reminiscent of one she would use in church, she said, "Does that mean we're getting married?"

Kevin laughed and pulled her up to his chest for a massive hug. "Yeah, *piccolina,* we're getting married."

"With a big outdoor wedding at Kevin's house in Riverside." Sam couldn't help it. The devil on her shoulder poked and prodded and the words were out before she could stop them.

Kevin snapped his head around so fast his neck cracked.

When he saw the smile on her face and the wicked gleam in her eyes, he picked Michy up and sat her on the floor. "*Piccolina*, you get dressed for school. I have something to discuss with your mamma. Shut the door behind you, okay?"

As Michy slammed the door and pattered down the hallway toward her room, Kevin narrowed his eyes and snatched the covers off Sam. "That was uncalled for and will get you ten swats."

"Only ten? I thought for sure that was a twenty-lick offense." Crawling up his chest, she said, "I love you, Kevin Mazze. I look forward to a lifetime of jumping with you."

You've just finished reading *Crossing Lines (Heat Wave Novel #3)*. If you enjoyed this book, please help others discover it by leaving a review.

If you'd like to stay abreast of contests and new releases, please join my newsletter: www.alannahlynne.com/contact/
or follow me on
Facebook: facebook.com/AuthorAlannahLynne
Twitter: @alannahlynne
Tsu: www.tsu.co/AlannahLynne

Other books in the *Heat Wave* series are:

Saving Me (Heat Wave Novel #1)
Last Call (Heat Wave Novel #2)
Going All In (Heat Wave Novel #4)
A Matter of Time (Heat Wave Novel #5)

Each book in the *Heat Wave* series stands alone and can be read out of order.

Turn the page to read an excerpt from *Going All In (Heat Wave Novel #4)*.

Excerpt – GOING ALL IN – Heat Wave Novel #4

Chapter One

$\mathcal{A}$ sudden burst of cold air rushed through Wade Neumann's construction trailer office, tossing the papers on his desk into the air like confetti on Times Square Rockin' New Year's Eve. As they floated to the floor, his boss, Kevin Mazze, stomped his boots on the concrete block steps to knock off the mud, then stepped into the trailer and let the door slam shut behind him. The framed site plans hanging on the walls rattled from the force, as did Wade's teeth.

"Jesus Christ." Wade propped his elbows on top of his gray-metal desk and cradled his head in his hands. The viselike grip helped steady the sloshing brain cells and slightly reduced the throb in his temples but did nothing to lessen the rising tide in the pit of his stomach.

"Sorry, the wind caught the door before I could stop it from slamming."

Kevin Mazze, owner of Mazze Builders, wasn't just Wade's boss. He was also a close, personal friend. However, given Wade's current condition after having spent the past twenty-four hours with *friends,* he was considering the need for new, less rambunctious… kinder friends. Especially given the extra little twinkle emanating from Kevin's dark eyes and the shit-eating grin splitting his face. Bastard wasn't sorry. Hell, he wasn't even in the same time zone as sorry.

"I can tell. Your face shows how deeply pained and remorseful you truly are."

Kevin's booming laughter filled the air, and the chair across from Wade's desk squeaked with Kevin's weight as he took a seat.

Wade leaned over to pick up the papers but found keeping his head higher than his thumping heart to lessen the bass in his head was an impossible task. In an effort to minimize the impact as much as possible, he dove to the floor, scooped up the mess, and dumped it all in a pile on his desk. His own chair *thwumped* from the impact as he dropped back into it, then took a couple of deep breaths to fight off the pain and nausea brought on by the sudden movement.

"You must've had one hell of a night."

Without moving his head, Wade met Kevin's curious stare but didn't answer. Not because he didn't want his boss to know where he'd been or what he'd been doing, but the old heave-ho in his stomach made him fear more than words would fly out if he opened his mouth.

It didn't matter if he answered or not, though. Kevin was perfectly content to carry on the conversation by himself. "Let me guess"—he dropped his head back and stared at the ceiling—"Bernice the bartender?"

Wade let his heavy eyelids slam shut over his burning eyes, like shutters being drawn over storefront windows. He imagined hanging a CLOSED sign to the front of them with the hopes Mazze would get the subliminal message and go away or, at the very least, shut the hell up. However, in all the years he'd known Mazze, subtlety had never worked, so he didn't know why he thought it would now.

"Cathy at the Citgo?" After another no-comment from Wade, Mazze continued. "Sandy at the Strip?"

Sandy?

Wade cracked an eye and scrunched up his face. "Who the hell is—"

Kevin threw his head back with laughter. "Gotcha."

Unwilling to acknowledge Kevin *did* have two of the names right, or that his life had been reduced to a revolving door of women with names that sounded like they belonged in tongue-twisters, Wade sighed and grabbed his cup of strong-enough-to-double-as-a-heavy-duty-degreaser coffee and took a hefty gulp. Now he needed a plate of greasy eggs, potatoes, and a pound of bacon. All wouldn't be right with the world, but it'd sure look a hell of a lot better.

"It wasn't that kind of night." He took another hefty sip of the coffee and set it back on his desk. Probably best not to overindulge with anything this morning after last night's binge. "Tyler, Alex, and a few other guys from home are here for vacation. I spent the night at Huntington Beach State Park with them. Tyler brought some of his famous apple pie moonshine—"

The words caused a resurgence of flavor on his tongue and he swallowed deeply, forcing back the gurgle in his gut. After the wave of nausea passed, he said, "I don't think I'll ever be able to eat Grandma's apple pie again."

Kevin shook his head and chuckled.

If Wade's mom shook her head like that, he'd assume her thoughts were something like, *Where did I go wrong? What makes my reasonably intelligent son do such stupid things?* However, he imagined Kevin's thoughts were more like, *Damn, I miss the good old days.*

Wade had known Kevin for eight years and had lived with him for the first six months of their friendship. He'd been around long enough, seen enough, and heard enough stories to know Kevin wasn't a saint, and there wasn't anything Wade or his friends did that Kevin hadn't also done. Probably in multiple. But since marrying Sam and settling down, the guy had grown wings and sprouted a freaking halo. Against all odds, Wildman had been tamed.

"Erik and Steve are crazy," Kevin said, referring to his two best friends, "and we've done some ridiculous things over the years. But your boys are balls-to-the-wall crazy."

Wade shrugged. "That's mostly Tyler. The rest of us just like having a good time."

Right, 'cause feeling like he'd been put through a blender the next morning was soooo much fun.

Kevin's eyes narrowed. "Are you still drunk?"

"I'd give my left nut to still be drunk. Unfortunately, I'm not. I switched to water early"—early being two—"so I could make it to work this morning."

He might be an idiot, but at least he was responsible.

"I'm more tired than anything." Well, except for the pounding headache and the possible regurgitation issues. "I poured myself into my sleeping bag around four, but they were still going strong, so I didn't get much sleep."

"They didn't bring a camper this year?"

Wade rubbed the back of his neck and grinned. He knew where this line of questioning would lead, but there wasn't any stopping it now. "No, and I wasn't about to spoon with Tyler in his tent, so I slept in my sleeping bag under the stars."

Mazze cranked his head around and watched the rain blow sideways against the window. "You must've been doing more than moonshine to see stars." This time when he shook his head, Wade figured his thoughts were more closely aligned with disappointed parent than jealous friend. "Not only has it been raining most of the night, but the temperature got down to thirty, *and* we have gale warnings." Another shake of the head. "And you say you're not bat-shit crazy."

Wade scrubbed a hand over his face. "Okay, I wasn't under the stars. I was under the tailgate of my truck. And I'm not crazy, just country."

"Country folks everywhere should be insulted." Mazze studied him from the corner of his eye. "Seriously, are you okay to drive? Legally?"

"Yeah, I'm fine."

To prove a point, or maybe just to prove he was an ass, Kevin crossed his foot over his knee and, in the process, kicked the shit out of the front of Wade's metal desk with his heavy work boot. The sound reverberated off the paneled walls and collided with a resounding clang in the middle of Wade's head, forcing him to grab his skull and hold on for dear life.

"Shit, what did Sam do to put you in such an evil mood? You're not normally this big of a dick; it must've been extreme." Kevin didn't answer the rhetorical question, so with the gong still echoing in his ears, Wade amended his previous answer. "I'm fine to drive. Where do you need me to go?"

Sighing, Kevin watched the rain fill the concrete forms where the circular driveway and sidewalk were supposed to be poured today. As foreman, Wade oversaw the day-to-day operations of specific Mazze Builders' projects, while Kevin took care of the big-picture items on all Mazze Builders' jobs. Because of his busy schedule, Kevin didn't get many opportunities to play in the dirt. He'd been looking forward to helping Wade finish up the last few items on their punch list so they could get The Chesapeake—Mazze Builders' latest golf course community—open.

Mother Nature, however, had other plans. Regardless of their time crunch and the need to finish the concrete work so Wade could get their Certificate of Occupancy, they weren't finishing today. The only thing currently on Wade's agenda was finishing up last week's paperwork so Marianne, Kevin's sister and Mazze Builders' office manager, could do payroll. After that, he was headed home for a much-needed nap.

"Since we're obviously not moving forward here today, I need you to go over to The Bellamy and help Callie finish the staging in the clubhouse. The open house is next week. At least we can get one property up and running and generating revenue."

Hearing Callie's name caused Wade to stiffen as if he'd been hit by an all-over body cramp. The last thing he wanted to do, today or any other day, was work with the uptight princess again. The first time they worked together, she made it clear he was far beneath her station in life. She successfully managed to make one of the worst periods of Wade's life—the week following his broken engagement—nearly unbearable.

God, it had been over a year, but he still remembered it like it was yesterday. Salt in open wounds tended to leave a long-lasting impression. They'd been in the final stages of the Vanguard development—Wade's first job as foreman—and as a favor to a client, Kevin brought Callie in for an interview. She suggested ways to stage the clubhouse and sales office for their grand opening, and, just his shitty luck, Kevin and Marianne loved her ideas.

They hired her on the spot and the next thing he knew, he was working with a clone of his ex. Not only did she physically resemble Miranda, but she had an identical attitude—that of a spoiled-rotten, self-absorbed daddy's girl. She treated him like a set of hands, arms, and legs that were great for moving furniture, but he had nothing above the neck worth paying attention to. As far as she was concerned, he was the puppet, there to serve her every need, and she was the master. The craziest part was she didn't even seem to enjoy pulling the damned strings. She was one of the most uptight individuals he'd ever met, and if he never had to work with her again, it would be too soon.

His throat clogged with a million arguments as to why he couldn't go, but he pressed his lips together and held them in check. His and Kevin's personal relationship often entailed a lot of joking, much like this morning, and Kevin was the brother he never had. But Kevin was also his boss, and Wade had a ton of respect for the guy. For that reason, he kept his bitter comments locked behind sealed lips.

He considered calling one of his crewmen to go do Callie's bidding, but they'd all worked a ton of overtime and weekends lately and were enjoying a rare day off. He couldn't bring himself to shit on their parade, just to save himself a little discomfort. He looked at his watch. *Eight thirty.* She probably hadn't even rolled out of her pedestal bed yet, so hopefully he'd have time for another pot of coffee and a greasy meal before dancing with the devil. "What time do I need to be there?"

Kevin grinned and shoved to his feet. "As soon as you can. Callie's on her way now."

The coffee—or maybe the dregs of the moonshine—bubbled up. He glanced at the papers on his desk, then curled his lip in what he hoped projected a relaxed smile and positive attitude. "Okay. I'll get these timecards signed and over to Marianne, then head that way."

"Good." Kevin paused with his hand on the door handle and glanced over his shoulder. His normal laidback, happy-go-lucky demeanor melted into an uncharacteristically serious glare. "Be nice to Callie."

Huh?

Kevin's tone was flat and sharp as a knife's edge. "I know she favors her, but she's not Miranda. She's actually a sweet girl, and you need to stop being an ass." As an exclamation point to the directive, he stomped down the steps and let the door slam shut behind him like a warning shot.

Wade wanted to yell out the window that there wasn't anything sweet about Callie Holden, but rather than act like a toddler trying to get in the last word against a scolding parent, he took off his favorite Georgia Bulldogs cap and ran his free hand over the top of his head.

After their last dance, rather than being a little bitch and running off to tell Kevin Callie should be named Cruella, he kept his head down, did his job, and focused on their mutual goal of getting the property ready to open. And after they finished the project, he made sure he never had to deal with her again.

Until today.

"Fine," he growled to the empty space around him.

He'd been through worse and survived. At least this time, he wasn't trying to keep the pieces of his obliterated heart from falling out of his chest while working, so he could go in, get shit done, and get out. He didn't know how much she'd already finished, but he thought she'd been working there for a couple of days. With any luck, he'd be done by lunch and headed home for his much-needed nap.

Going All In (Heat Wave Novel #4) – Available now!

www.ingramcontent.com/pod-product-compliance
Lightning Source LLC
Chambersburg PA
CBHW022015170626
46808CB00001B/421